As You Like It

A Musical Adaptation of
William Shakespeare's
As You Like It

Adapted by
Shaina Taub and
Laurie Woolery

Music and Lyrics by
Shaina Taub

concord
theatricals

FOR PRODUCTION INQUIRIES

UNITED STATES AND CANADA
info@concordtheatricals.com
1-866-979-0447

UNITED KINGDOM AND EUROPE
licensing@concordtheatricals.co.uk
020-7054-7298

Each title is subject to availability from Concord Theatricals Corp., depending upon country of performance. Please be aware that *AS YOU LIKE IT* may not be licensed by Concord Theatricals Corp. in your territory. Professional and amateur producers should contact the nearest Concord Theatricals Corp. office or licensing partner to verify availability.

No one shall make any changes in this title(s) for the purpose of production. No part of this book may be reproduced, stored in a retrieval system, scanned, uploaded, or transmitted in any form, by any means, now known or yet to be invented, including mechanical, electronic, digital, photocopying, recording, videotaping, or otherwise, without the prior written permission of the publisher. No one shall share this title(s), or any part of this title(s), through any social media or file hosting websites.

For all inquiries regarding motion picture, television, online/digital and other media rights, please contact Concord Theatricals Corp.

THIRD-PARTY MATERIALS USE NOTE

Licensees are solely responsible for obtaining formal written permission from copyright owners to use copyrighted third-party materials (e.g., incidental music not provided in connection with a performance license, artworks, logos) in the performance of this play and are strongly cautioned to do so. If no such permission is obtained by the licensee, then the licensee must use only original materials and materials that the licensee owns and controls. Licensees are solely responsible and liable for clearances of all third-party copyrighted materials, and shall indemnify the copyright owners of the play(s) and their licensing agent, Concord Theatricals Corp., against any costs, expenses, losses and liabilities arising from the use of such copyrighted third-party materials by licensees. For music, please contact the appropriate music licensing authority in your territory for the rights to any incidental music not provided in connection with a performance license.

IMPORTANT BILLING AND CREDIT REQUIREMENTS

If you have obtained performance rights to this title, please refer to your licensing agreement for important billing and credit requirements.

AS YOU LIKE IT was originally commissioned and produced by The Public Theater (Oskar Eustis, Artistic Director; Patrick Willingham, Executive Director) and opened at the Delacorte Theater in Central Park, New York, on September 1, 2017. The performance was directed by Laurie Woolery, with choreography by Sonya Tayeh, scenic design by David Rockwell, costume design by Andrea Hood, lighting design by David Weiner, sound design by Jessica Paz, and orchestrations by Mike Brun. The Production Stage Manager was Michael Domue. The cast was as follows:

JAQUES	Shaina Taub
ORLANDO	Ato Blankson-Wood
OLIVER	Marc Randolph Henry
ROSALIND	Rebecca Naomi Jones
CELIA	Idania Quezada
TOUCHSTONE	Joel Perez
DUKE SENIOR	Darius De Haas
DUKE FREDERICK	Antoine Jones
SILVIA	Ariel Mapp
PHOEBE	Mayelyn Perdomo
ANDY	Troy Anthony
ADAM	William Anderson
ANNOUNCER	Daniel Hall
REFEREE	Patrick O'Hare
BRONCO'S AGENT	Lori Brown-Niang
PAPA CORIN	Eddie Bottoms
MAMA CORIN	Dorothy Vazquez
WILLIAM	Matthew Vazquez
MARTEXT	Catherine Watson
HISPERIA	Sue Newman
MISS AMIENS	Vivian Jett
YOUNG GIRL	Naomi Pierre
BRONCO, FRANKIE FLOW & CAVEMAN	Bronx Wrestling Federation
WEDDING DANCERS	Freedom Dabka Group
WEDDING SINGERS	The Sing Harlem Choir
ARDENITE DRUM CIRCLE	Harambee Dance Company

FEATURED DANCERS . . . . Dezire Duverglas, Genesis Perdomo, Adi Présumé, Keila Ramos, Nourah Nadege Sidibe, Annie Zhao

ROYAL MINIONS . . . . .Nelson Chimilio, Jennifer Levine, Madeline Ramos, Shannon Rhett, Michael Roberts, Benjamin Solotaire, James P. Stanton

ATTENDANTS . . . . .Hasaan Bailey, Kelly Campbell, Clarimar Capellan, Bianca Edwards, Nanya-Akuki Goodrich, Vivian Kogan, Natalie Pierre, Nisani Walser, Ryan Washington

PUPPETEERS. . . . . Sarah Bernero, Llewellyn "LC" Connolly, Tenaya Griffin, Anthony Michael Parmer

ARDENITES/COURT CITIZENS . . . . .Tamara Pilar Allen, Noemi Avenancio, Thomas Barzey, Louise Bynoe, Chris Campbell, Cinthia Candelaria, Janet Cardona, Carlson Clarke, Micarla Clarke, Michelle Clarke, Brenda Coker, Enmanuelle "Manny" Collado, Chanel Corcino, Joycelyn Cunningham, Nyesha Davis, Cora Dennis, Rosa Downing, Laura Dukes, Ellie Dunn, Suzie Dunn, Gladys Ellington, Ella Evans, Rajeeyah Finnie-Myers, Zion Finnie-Myers, Aileen Fraser, Pinnacle Garcia, Angelica Gaussaint, Giovanna Gordon, Pierre Graves, Althia Haynes, Sherese Hoover, Alma Hueston, Fatemata Krubally, Evelyn Leary, Aynisa Leonardo, Lucia Mason, Muriel Moses, Aden Munassar, Ziara Naranjo, Abraham Nasher, Edali Nuñez, Beluvid Ola-Jendai, Alizah Olivo, Josiah Olivo, Nelson Olivo, Soriah Olivo, Lizeth Palencia, Louise Parks, Virginia Perry, Eric Pierre, Nancy Hannah Pierre, Nancy Pierre, Ka Keith Puan, Anabelle Ramos, Mike Ramos, Gloria Ranjitsingh, Angelina Rivera, Marcia Rose, Bruce Rutherford, Alfreda Small, Denton Alexander "Lex" Smith, David Smith, Paul "P-Funk" Stallings, Roslyn Svendsen, Eirene Tuakora, Sanira Walser, Sally Ann Williams, Samantha Williams, Yuan Ming Zhao

AS YOU LIKE IT was remounted at the Delacorte Theater, opening on August 10, 2022. The performance was directed by Laurie Woolery, with scenic design by Myung Hee Cho, costume design by Emilio Sosa, lighting design by Isabella Byrd, sound design by Sun Hee Kil, and orchestrations by Mike Brun. The Production Stage Manager was Kristen Gibbs. The cast was as follows:

JAQUES	Shaina Taub
ORLANDO	Ato Blankson-Wood
OLIVER	Renrick Palmer
ROSALIND	Rebecca Naomi Jones
CELIA	Idania Quezada
TOUCHSTONE	Christopher M. Ramirez
DUKE SENIOR	Darius De Haas
DUKE FREDERICK	Eric Pierre
SILVIA	Brianna Cabrera
PHOEBE	Bianca Edwards
ANDY	Jonathan Jordan
ADA (RED ENSEMBLE)	Monica Patricia Davis
ADA (BLUE ENSEMBLE)	Alfreda Small
ANNOUNCER (RED ENSEMBLE)	Melissa Apedo
ANNOUNCER (BLUE ENSEMBLE)	Sandy "Goldie" Randall
REFEREE (RED ENSEMBLE)	Tommy Williams
REFEREE (BLUE ENSEMBLE)	Jason Asher
AGENT	Lori Brown-Niang
PAPA CORIN (RED ENSEMBLE)	Eddie Bottoms
PAPA CORIN (BLUE ENSEMBLE)	Philip Milio
MAMA CORIN (RED ENSEMBLE)	Dorothy Vazquez
MAMA CORIN (BLUE ENSEMBLE)	Rose Bullen
WILLIAM	Damion Allen
MARTEXT (RED ENSEMBLE)	Eileen Chen
MARTEXT (BLUE ENSEMBLE)	Zi Ling Wu
HISPERIA (RED ENSEMBLE)	Marcia Rose
HISPERIA (BLUE ENSEMBLE)	Theresa Middleton
MISS AMIENS	Vivian Jett Brown
LITTLE JAQUES (RED ENSEMBLE)	Noemi Avenancio
LITTLE JAQUES (BLUE ENSEMBLE)	Naomi Pierre
LUCHA LIBRE WRESTLERS	Bronx Wrestling Federation
JAQUES STANDBY	Emily Gardner Xu Hall

UNDERSTUDIES . . . Amar Atkins, Sean-Michael Bruno, Danyel Fulton, Asha Jené, Trevor McGhie, Mike Millán, Marcia Rose, Kevin Tate, Claudia Yanez

ARDEN DANCERS . . . . Fiona Chen, Pierre Graves, Bobby Moody, Nancy Hannah Pierre, Genesis Perdomo Santos

DE BOYS DANCERS . . . . Tristan André, Pierre Harmony Graves, Bobby Moody, Edwin Rivera

ROYAL MINIONS (RED ENSEMBLE) . . . . Philip Browning, Joel Frost, Maddie Ramos, Holly Valentine, Nicholas Watson, Sally Ann Williams

ROYAL MINIONS (BLUE ENSEMBLE) . . . . Nelson Chimilio, Julie Geisler, Lanisha Javon Gholston, Jennifer Levine, Shannon Rhett, James P. Stanton

LADIES-IN-WAITING . . . . Clarimar Capellan, Fiona Chen, Nancy Hannah Pierre, Genesis Perdomo Santos, Mili Shrestha, Angel Universe

ATTENDANTS . . . . Tristan André, Clarimar Capellan, Reina Celis, Edwin Rivera, Mili Shrestha, Angel Universe

PUPPET-DEERS . . . . .Lori Brown-Niang, Maria Capellan, Sabrina Cedeño, Nanjean Gonzalez, Eric Herrera, Jonpaul Niang, Arianne Recto

ARDENITES/ROYAL SUBJECTS (RED ENSEMBLE) . . . . Tymala Apedo, Janet Cardona, Cheryl Chen, Liming Chen, Kenneth Collins, Joycelyn Cunningham, Laura Dukes, Ella Evans, Nestor "Pana" Eversley, Zoë Frost, Alma Hueston, Naomi Leimsider, Christine Y. Lewis, Doreen McGill, Aidan Naranjo-Sosa, Sarahi Naranjo-Sosa, Ziara Naranjo-Sosa, Amy Ponce, Armani Ponce, Martina Ramirez, Chamaine Smith, Roslyn Svendsen, Noah Terrell, Magdalen Wilson, Tina Ye

ARDENITES/ROYAL SUBJECTS (BLUE ENSEMBLE) . . . . .Xiao Xia Cai, Suzie Celis, Jessica Cermak, Chloe Chen, Irene Chen, Stephanie Chen, Gladys Ellington, Almostafa "Mustafa" Elnoor, Zion Finnie-Myers, Faith Harper, Guadalupe Herrera, Ervin "Easy" Hunt, Aaron Williams Knight, Fatemata Krubally, Susan Lin, Daniel Martinez, Olivia Murphy, Lizeth Palencia, Nancy Pierre, Sheila Roberson, Suzzette Rose, Xiu Feng Shi, Chontay "Chon" Smith, Sheree Watson, Shoshana M.F. Waves, Lin Feng Wu

CHARACTERS

Cast Size

5 principal women, 6 principal men, many featured roles cast from an ensemble of flexible size.

PRINCIPALS

JAQUES – a young philosopher/writer

ORLANDO – the orphan son of Sir Rowland de Boys and younger brother to Oliver

OLIVER – Orlando's older brother

ROSALIND – daughter of Duke Senior

CELIA – Rosalind's cousin, daughter of Duke Frederick

TOUCHSTONE – a clown

DUKE SENIOR – a banished duke, Rosalind's father

DUKE FREDERICK – the new duke, Celia's father

SILVIA – a shepherdess

PHOEBE – a shepherdess

ANDY – a farmhand

FEATURED ROLES

(should be double/triple cast from within the ensemble)

YOUNG ROSALIND – a child

YOUNG ORLANDO – a child

TWEEN ROSALIND – a tween

TWEEN ORLANDO – a tween

ADAM – an elderly, longtime employee of the de Boys estate

ANNOUNCER – a hype man for the wrestling match

REFEREE – for the wrestling match

BRONCO'S AGENT – a high-powered sports agent

PAPA CORIN – a farmer

MAMA CORIN – the farmer's wife

WILLIAM – a local farmer in Arden

MARTEXT – an Ardenite priestess

HISPERIA – a nosy lady-in-waiting to Celia

MISS AMIENS – a soulful honky tonk singer in Arden

BRONCO – the reigning Lucha Libre champion

FRANKIE FLOW – a Lucha Libre wrestler

CAVEMAN – a Lucha Libre wrestler

GRANDMA ROSALIND – an elder

GRANDPA ORLANDO – an elder

LITTLE JAQUES – a young girl with ideas

Note: The characters of Bronco, Frankie Flow, and Caveman were inspired by real Lucha Libre wrestlers from the Bronx Wrestling Federation who performed in the original Public Works production in Central Park. If you would like to know more about them, you can visit their Facebook, Instagram, or X page.

ENSEMBLE

Ensemble size is flexible.

ROYAL SUBJECTS

ARDENITES – a diverse community of refugees

DE BOYS DANCERS – members of the boy band DE BOYS

ROYAL MINIONS – (minimum two, maximum: however many you want!) loyal court members and council to Duke Frederick

LADIES-IN-WAITING – for Celia and Rosalind

ATTENDANTS – Duke Senior's inner circle

PUPPET-DEERS – the wildlife in Arden

HUNTERS – in Arden

SETTING

The action of this play takes place now and always in a kingdom surrounded by a forest called Arden. Arden is the mythical sanctuary where we all need to travel in order to heal. Arden is here, there, and everywhere. No one is an expert in our Arden.

As You Like It is intended to be performed in one act, without an intermission.

AUTHORS' NOTES

AS YOU LIKE IT is part of a vibrant canon of new American musicals originally created for Public Works, a radically inclusive program at The Public Theater that believes "Culture belongs to everyone."

Yes, we originally performed it at the Delacorte Theater with over 200 New Yorkers, including actual Lucha Libre wrestlers, a teen gospel choir, African drummers, Dabka wedding dancers, and a community puppeteer group, but we also wanted to make sure we created a vibrant and robust adaptation that could be performed with a cast as small as fifteen in a blackbox.

We invite you to participate in this movement by staging our *AS YOU LIKE IT* with your communities, school groups, and institutions across the country and around the globe. It's flexible and can be produced as a straight-up musical or you can explode it open by adding large numbers of people. Just as Shakespeare's plays did in their time, our goal is to reflect the world we are living in now and invite all citizens into the creative experience. Our Arden is filled with different musical styles in order to create as inclusive a world as possible.

For those who are interested in putting on large-scale community pageant-style productions of *AS YOU LIKE IT* and would like more information on Public Works' model for community engagement, The Public Theater's website features information on the Public Works program.

AS YOU LIKE IT is dedicated to our community.

MUSICAL NUMBERS

Scene One
Prologue

*(**JAQUES**, a philosopher, with pen and paper in hand, is working on an unfinished philosophy. She is never without her pen and paper.)*

[MUSIC 01 – PROLOGUE: ALL THE WORLD'S A STAGE]

JAQUES.
ALL THE WORLD'S A STAGE,
AND EV'RYBODY'S IN THE SHOW.
NOBODY'S A PRO.
ALL THE WORLD'S A STAGE,
AND EV'RY DAY, WE PLAY OUR PART,
ACTING OUT OUR HEART.
YEAR BY YEAR, WE GROW,
LEARNING AS WE GO,
TRYIN' TO TELL A STORY WE CAN FEEL.
HOW DO YOU MAKE THE MAGIC REAL?

*(**YOUNG ROSALIND** and **YOUNG ORLANDO** enter, accompanied by their parents.)*

DA DA DA DA DA DA DA,
DA DA DA DA DA DA DA,
DA DA DA DA DA DA DA DA DA DA DA.

WE START AS BABIES,
BORN UNAFRAID TO CRY,
PUKING ON OUR PARENTS' SHIRTS,
STILL STARING UP WITH WONDER AT THE SKY.

JAQUES.
AND THEN WE'RE KIDS,
NOT YET CAPABLE OF HATE,
FREELY DANCING WITH EACH OTHER,
UNAWARE INSIDE OUR YOUTH
OF A DIFF'RENCE BETWEEN MAKE-BELIEVE AND TRUTH.

(Their parents fade away, leaving the two **YOUNG KIDS** *alone.)*

YOUNG ROSALIND & YOUNG ORLANDO.
ALL THE WORLD'S A STAGE,

JAQUES.
DA DA DA DA DA DA DA,

YOUNG ROSALIND & YOUNG ORLANDO.
ALL THE WORLD'S A STAGE,

JAQUES.
DA DA DA DA DA DA DA.

*(***YOUNG ROSALIND*** and ***YOUNG ORLANDO*** grow a little older and are replaced by* **TWEEN ROSALIND** *and* **TWEEN ORLANDO.***)*

THEN WE GET BIGGER,
AND THINK BEFORE WE PLAY.
GIVE EACH OTHER STAGE FRIGHT,
AND WORRY WHAT THE CRITICS HAVE TO SAY.

WE HIDE IN COSTUME,
PRETEND WE BLEND IN WITH THE SCENERY,
AND ACT THE WAY WE'RE TAUGHT WE OUGHTA BE.

TWEEN ROSALIND & TWEEN ORLANDO.
ALL THE WORLD'S A STAGE,

JAQUES.
DA DA DA DA DA DA DA,

TWEEN ROSALIND & TWEEN ORLANDO.
ALL THE WORLD'S A STAGE,

JAQUES.
DA DA DA DA DA DA

(**TWEEN ROSALIND** *and* **TWEEN ORLANDO** *grow into young adults and are replaced by our* **ROSALIND** *and* **ORLANDO.***)*

THEN WE'RE ALMOST GROWN-UPS
TRYIN' TO FILL OUR PARENTS' SHOES
WITH BROKEN SOLES.
WE QUESTION OUR ROLES,
CAN'T SEEM TO FIND OUR LIGHT,
SICK OF WAITING IN THE WINGS OF THE SAME LIFE
NIGHT AFTER NIGHT,
LONGING FOR A DUET
WITH SOMEONE WHO TRULY SEES YOU.
WE DON'T KNOW THE WORDS YET,
BUT WE'LL SING UNTIL WE DO.

ALL THE WORLD'S A STAGE,
AND EV'RYBODY'S IN THE SHOW.
NOBODY'S A PRO.
ALL THE WORLD'S A STAGE,
AND EV'RY DAY, WE PLAY OUR PART,
ACTING OUT OUR HEART.
YEAR BY YEAR, WE GROW,
LEARNING AS WE GO,
TRYIN' TO TELL A STORY WE CAN FEEL.
HOW DO YOU MAKE THE MAGIC REAL?
HOW DO YOU MAKE THE MAGIC REAL?

(*They exit.*)

End of Scene

Scene Two
The De Boys Estate

*(The **ROYAL MINIONS** enter.)*

[MUSIC 01A – HEAR YE, HEAR YE]

ROYAL MINIONS.
AH AH AH
ALL HAIL DUKE FRED'RICK!
AH AH AH
ALL HAIL DUKE FRED'RICK!

A ROYAL MINION. Hear ye! Hear ye!

A ROYAL MINION. The new Duke Frederick's royal wrestling tournament shall commence tonight!

A ROYAL MINION. All royal subjects of the court must attend!

*(The **ROYAL MINIONS** exit.)*

[MUSIC 02 – THE MAN I'M SUPPOSED TO BE]

*(**ORLANDO** enters, practicing his moves for the upcoming wrestling match.)*

(He counts his reps as he goes.)

ORLANDO.
ONE, TWO, THREE – HUH!
ONE, TWO, THREE – HUH!

*(Enter **ADAM**, an elderly longtime employee of the de Boys estate.)*

ADAM. Orlando, yonder comes my master, your brother Oliver.

ORLANDO. Go apart, Adam, and thou shalt hear how he will shake me up. He bars me the place of a brother, and this is it that grieves me.

(**ADAM** *exits.*)

THE LAST THING OUR DAD DID BEFORE HE DIED
WAS TELL MY BROTHER TO RAISE ME RIGHT.
HE MADE HIM SWEAR TO SUPPORT ME AND SCHOOL ME,
'CAUSE HE'D BE THE MAN OF THE HOUSE NOW,
BUT MY BROTHER, HE BROKE THAT VOW.

HE'S KEPT ME IN THE DARK IN THIS ROTTEN PLACE
WITH ONLY MY TAIL TO CHASE,
LIKE A PIG IN HIS PEN.
AN ANIMAL, NOT A MAN.

NOW I'M GROWN AND I'VE GOT NO JOB, NO DEGREE,
SO NO ONE TAKES ME SERIOUSLY.
JUST ANOTHER UNEDUCATED PUNK WITH NO SHOT.
BUT I'M NOT,
AND SOON, THEY'LL SEE

I AM THE SON OF SIR ROWLAND DE BOYS!
AND HIS SPIRIT GROW, GROW, GROWS IN ME.
AND I'M THE ONLY ONE WHO CAN LIVE UP TO
HIS BRAVE AND RIGHTEOUS NAME!
I AM THE SON OF SIR ROWLAND DE BOYS!
AND HIS SPIRIT SHOW, SHOW, SHOWS IN ME.
SO BROTHER, BETTER BEWARE.
I'M BECOMING THE MAN I'M SUPPOSED TO BE.
THE MAN I'M SUPPOSED TO, SUPPOSED TO BE.

ONE, TWO, THREE.
'CAUSE HARD AS HE TRIED TO SHUT ME INSIDE,
HE COULDN'T STOP ME FROM MAKING STRIDES.
HE MAY HAVE INHERITED HIS MONEY,
BUT (*HUH!*) I GOT HIS SKILLS. (*HA!*)
AND I'VE TRAINED MYSELF DAY AND NIGHT.
YEAH, I'VE BEEN GETTING READY TO FIGHT.
AND I'M FINALLY STRONG ENOUGH
TO MAN UP, STAND UP,
RIP ALL HIS COMMANDS UP
TIL HE'LL RECOGNIZE

ORLANDO.
I AM THE SON OF SIR ROWLAND DE BOYS!
AND HIS SPIRIT FLOW, FLOW, FLOWS IN ME.
SO BROTHER, BETTER BEWARE.
I'M BECOMING THE MAN I'M SUPPOSED TO BE.
THE MAN I'M SUPPOSED TO, SUPPOSED TO

TONIGHT, WHEN I WRESTLE IN THE CHAMPIONSHIP,
I'M GONNA EARN THE HONOR
I'VE BEEN NEEDING FOR SO LONG.
I'M GONNA PROVE THEIR VERSION OF ME WRONG.
I'M GONNA MAKE THE WHOLE WORLD UNDERSTAND.
IF ONLY SOMEONE WOULD UNDERSTAND!

(Enter **ADAM** *and* **OLIVER**, *Orlando's older brother.)*

OLIVER. Now, sir, what make you here?

ORLANDO. Nothing. I am not taught to make anything.

OLIVER. What mar you then, sir?

ORLANDO. I am helping you to mar that which God made, a poor unworthy brother of yours, with idleness.

OLIVER. Know you where you are, sir?

ORLANDO. O, sir, very well.

OLIVER. Know you before whom, sir?

ORLANDO. I have as much of my father in me as you!

OLIVER. What, boy!

(The **BROTHERS** *physically fight.)*

ORLANDO. Come, come, elder brother!

ADAM. Sweet brothers, be patient!

OLIVER. Wilt thou lay hands on me, villain?

ORLANDO. I am no villain!

I AM THE SON OF SIR ROWLAND DE BOYS!
AND HIS SPIRIT GROW, GROW, GROWS IN ME.
AND I WILL NOT ENDURE YOUR TORTURE
ONE MORE GOD-FORSAKEN DAY.
I AM THE SON OF SIR ROWLAND DE BOYS!
AND EVERYONE WILL KNOW, KNOW KNOW IT'S ME
'CAUSE STARTING TONIGHT, I'M BECOMING THE
MAN I'M SUPPOSED TO...
BROTHER, BEWARE
OF THE MAN THAT YOU'RE CLOSE TO.
YOU BETTER MAKE WAY FOR THE MAN I'M
SUPPOSED TO BE!

OLIVER. Well sir, get you in. I will not long be troubled with you.

(**ORLANDO** *exits.*)

Holla Adam! Was not Bronco, the duke's wrestler, here to speak with me?

ADAM. So please you, his agent is here at the door.

OLIVER. Call her in.

(*Enter* **BRONCO'S AGENT**, *a high powered sports agent.*)

AGENT. Good morrow to your Worship.

OLIVER. Good madam, what's the new news at the new court?

AGENT. There's no news at the court sir, but the old news. That is, the old Duke Senior is banished by his younger brother, the new Duke Frederick.

OLIVER. Can you tell if Duke Senior's daughter Rosalind be banished with her father?

AGENT. Oh, no, for Frederick's daughter, her cousin Celia, so loves Rosalind, that she would have followed her into exile or have died to stay behind her. Rosalind is at the court.

OLIVER. Where will the old Duke Senior live?

AGENT. They say he is already in the Forest of Arden, and a many merry people with him.

OLIVER. What, Bronco wrestles tonight at the court before the new Duke Frederick?

AGENT. Marry, does he, sir, and I came to acquaint you with a matter. I am given, sir, secretly to understand that your younger brother, Orlando, hath a disposition to come in disguised against Bronco to try a fall. Your brother is but young and tender, and, for your love, Bronco would be loath to foil him, as he must for his own honor if Orlando come in.

OLIVER. I'll tell thee: it is the stubbornest young fellow, full of ambition, and envious emulator of every man's good parts, a secret and villainous contriver against me, his natural brother. Therefore, tell Bronco: use his discretion. I had as lief he didst break his neck as his finger.

AGENT. If he come tonight, Bronco shall give him his payment.

OLIVER. Farewell, good madam.

(**BRONCO'S AGENT** *exits.*)

[MUSIC 02A – THE MAN I'M SUPPOSED TO BE (UNDERSCORE)]

(*To himself.*) I hope I shall see an end of my brother, for my soul – yet I know not why – hates nothing more than he. But it shall not be long, this wrestling shall clear all.

(*He exits.*)

End of Scene

Scene Three
Rosalind's Dressing Chamber

(**ROSALIND**, *a young noblewoman, in her underclothes. She is with her cousin* **CELIA**.)

CELIA. I pray thee, Rosalind, sweet my coz, be merry!

ROSALIND. Dear Celia, I show more mirth than I am mistress of, and would you yet I were merrier? Unless you could teach me how to forget a banished father, you must not learn me how to remember any extraordinary pleasure.

CELIA. If my uncle, thy banished father, had banished thy uncle, the Duke my father, so thou hadst been still with me, I could have taught my love to take thy father for mine.

ROSALIND. Well, I will forget the condition of my estate to rejoice in yours.

CELIA. What my father hath taken away from thy father perforce, I will render thee again in affection. Therefore, my sweet Rosalind, my dear Rose, be merry!

[MUSIC 03 – ROSALIND, BE MERRY]

(*Throughout this song,* **HISPERIA** *and the other* **LADIES-IN-WAITING** *dress* **ROSALIND** *in an elaborate gown, crown, and make-up.*)

ROSALIND.
ROSALIND, BE MERRY.
ROSALIND, BE BRIGHT.
EVEN THOUGH YOUR HEART IS BREAKING,
ACT LIKE YOU'RE ALRIGHT.

ROSALIND, BE PLEASANT.
ROSALIND, AGREE.
ROSALIND, JUST PLAY THE GIRL
THAT YOU'RE SUPPOSED TO BE.

ROSALIND.

> ROSALIND, BE ROSY.
> ROSALIND, BE GAY.
> ROSALIND, DON'T SPEAK
> UNLESS YOU'VE SOMETHING NICE TO SAY.
>
> ROSALIND, GET READY.
> IT'S NEARLY TIME TO GO.
> DRESS UP LIKE A PUPPET
> AND PUT ON ANOTHER SHOW.
>
> IF THEY ONLY KNEW
> WHAT'S UNDERNEATH THE COSTUME,
> UNDERNEATH THE COSTUME.
>
> ROSALIND, BE LOVELY.
> SMILE, WON'T YOU DEAR?
> YOU'LL MESS UP YOUR MAKE-UP
> IF YOU SHED ANOTHER TEAR.
>
> COVER UP YOUR SADNESS
> TUCK IT IN YOUR BRA.
> IT MAKES US UNCOMFORTABLE
> WHEN WOMEN HAVE A FLAW.
>
> ROSALIND, BE SIMPLE.
> ROSALIND, BE SMALL.
> DON'T YOU DARE TO HOPE
> FOR FREAKING ANYTHING AT ALL.
>
> ROSALIND, DON'T LOSE IT.
> ROSALIND, DON'T SWEAR.
> PAIN AND GRIEF AND RAGE ARE NOT
> APPROPRIATE TO WEAR.
>
> TONIGHT AT THE GAMES
> YOU WILL NOD AND APPLAUD
> LIKE A GOOD LITTLE FRAUD.
>
> MY GOD,
> IF THEY ONLY KNEW

WHAT'S UNDERNEATH THE COSTUME,
UNDERNEATH THE COSTUME,
WHAT'S DYING TO COME OUT
FROM UNDERNEATH THIS COSTUME.

ROSALIND, BE CAREFUL.
KEEP YOURSELF IN CHECK.
BETTER NOT BREAK CHARACTER,
OR THEY COULD BREAK YOUR NECK.

> (**ROSALIND** *catches sight of herself, now all done up, in the mirror.*)

ROSALIND, BE HONEST.
TAKE A LOOK AND SEE.
IF YOU HAD NO ROLE TO PLAY,
THEN WHO WOULD YOU BE?

> (*Enter* **TOUCHSTONE***, a clown.*)

TOUCHSTONE. *(To* **CELIA***.)* Celia, you must come away to your father.

CELIA. Were you made the messenger, Touchstone?

TOUCHSTONE. No, by mine honor, but I was bid to come to you.

ROSALIND. Where learned you that oath, fool?

TOUCHSTONE. Of a certain knight that swore by his honor they were good pancakes, and swore by his honor the mustard was naught. Now, I'll stand to it, the pancakes were naught and the mustard was good, and yet was not the knight forsworn.

CELIA. How prove you that in the great heap of your knowledge?

ROSALIND. Ay, marry you unmuzzle your wisdom.

TOUCHSTONE. Stand you both forth now: stroke your chins and swear by your beards that I am a knave.

CELIA. By our beards (if we had them), thou art.

TOUCHSTONE. By my knavery (if I had it), then I were. But if you swear by that that is not, you are not forsworn. No more was this knight swearing by his honor, for he never had any; or if he had, he had sworn it away before ever he saw those pancakes or that mustard.

CELIA. Prithee, who is't that thou mean'st?

TOUCHSTONE. One that old Frederick, your father, loves.

CELIA. Speak no more of him, Touchstone; you'll be whipped for taxation one of these days.

TOUCHSTONE. The more pity that fools may not speak wisely what wise men do foolishly.

ROSALIND. For, since the little wit that fools have was silenced, the little foolery that wise men have makes a great show.

CELIA. Shall we see the wrestling, cousin?

TOUCHSTONE. You must if you stay here, for here is the place appointed for the wrestling, and they are ready to perform it!

(They exit.)

End of Scene

Scene Four
The Wrestling Ring

[MUSIC 04 – THE WRESTLING MATCH]

(A crowd of **ROYAL SUBJECTS** *enter, arriving at the arena for the games. They gather around a wrestling ring.)*

ANNOUNCER. Ladies and gentlemen, welcome to the Duke's royal wrestling championship! Are you ready?

ROYAL SUBJECTS. Yeah!

ANNOUNCER. *(Encouraging the audience to join in.)* I said, are you ready???

ROYAL SUBJECTS. YEAH!

ANNOUNCER. C'mon people, I can't hear you, I said ARE? YOU? READYYYYYY????

ROYAL SUBJECTS. YEAHHHHHH!!!!

ANNOUNCER. Ladies and Gentlemen, I present the Royal Duke Frederick!

(**DUKE FREDERICK** *enters with his entourage of* **ROYAL MINIONS.**)

(As he enters, all **SUBJECTS** *bow in fear.)*

ROYAL SUBJECTS & ROYAL MINIONS.
AH AH AH
ALL HAIL DUKE FRED'RICK!
AH AH AH
ALL HAIL DUKE FRED'RICK!

DUKE FREDERICK.
LET THE GAMES BEGIN!

ANNOUNCER. Round one! Introducing the undefeated, reigning champion: Bronco Internacional!

        *(***BRONCO**, *a masked lucha libre wrestler, enters and takes the ring.)*

ROYAL SUBJECTS.
    BRONCO, BRONCO! HE'S THE MAN!
    NO ONE CAN DO IT LIKE BRONCO CAN!
    BRONCO, BRONCO! HE'S THE MAN!
    NO ONE CAN DO IT LIKE BRONCO CAN!

ANNOUNCER. And his opponent: the fiery, the fearless Frankie Flow!

        *(***FRANKIE FLOW**, *another masked lucha libre wrestler, enters and takes the ring.)*

ROYAL SUBJECTS.
    FRANKIE FLOW'S THE MAN!
    FRANKIE FLOW'S THE MAN!
    IF ANYONE CAN BEAT HIM, FRANKIE CAN!
    FRANKIE FLOW'S THE MAN!
    FRANKIE FLOW'S THE MAN!
    IF ANYONE CAN BEAT HIM, FRANKIE CAN!

ANNOUNCER. Wrestlers, you shall try but one fall.

ANNOUNCER & ROYAL SUBJECTS.
    THREE! TWO! ONE! FIGHT!

        *(***BRONCO** *and* **FRANKIE FLOW** *wrestle!)*

ROYAL SUBJECTS.
    LET'S GO, BRONCO!
    LET'S GO FRANKIE!
    GO AND GET 'EM, WHOA!

    LET'S GO, BRONCO!
    LET'S GO FRANKIE!
    GO AND GET 'EM, WHOA!

    LET'S GO, BRONCO!
    LET'S GO FRANKIE!

GO AND GET 'EM, WHOA!
OOH! AH! OUCH! WOW!

(**BRONCO** *pins* **FRANKIE FLOW** *down.*)

REFEREE.
ONE, TWO, THREE!

ANNOUNCER.
AND THE WINNER IS BRONCO!

ALL.
WOO!

(**FRANKIE FLOW** *exits the ring.*)

ANNOUNCER. Round two! Bronco faces his second opponent: the primal, the vicious CAVEMAN!

(**CAVEMAN,** *another cameo masked Lucha Libre wrestler, enters and takes the ring.*)

ROYAL SUBJECTS.
CAVEMAN, CAVEMAN, HE'S THE MAN!
IF ANYONE CAN BEAT HIM, CAVEMAN CAN!
CAVEMAN, CAVEMAN, HE'S THE MAN!
IF ANYONE CAN BEAT HIM, CAVEMAN CAN!

ANNOUNCER. Wrestlers, you shall try but one fall.

ANNOUNCER & ROYAL SUBJECTS.
THREE, TWO, ONE! FIGHT!

(**BRONCO** *and* **CAVEMAN** *wrestle!*)

ROYAL SUBJECTS.
LET'S GO, BRONCO!
LET'S GO, CAVEMAN!
GO AND GET 'EM, WHOA!
LET'S GO, BRONCO!
LET'S GO, CAVEMAN!
GO AND GET 'EM, WHOA!

ROYAL SUBJECTS.
LET'S GO, BRONCO!
LET'S GO CAVEMAN!
GO AND GET 'EM, WHOA!
OOH! AH! OUCH! WOW!

(**BRONCO** *pins* **CAVEMAN** *down.*)

REFEREE.
ONE, TWO, THREE!

ANNOUNCER.
AND THE WINNER IS BRONCO AGAIN!

ALL.
WOO!

(**CAVEMAN** *exits the ring.*)

ANNOUNCER.   Round three – the last round for the championship! Bronco faces his third and final opponent...

(*Reading from a slip of paper.*)

...Orlando?

(**ORLANDO** *enters the ring in a mask as the crowd murmurs.*)

A ROYAL SUBJECT.
WHO IS THIS KID?

A ROYAL SUBJECT.
HE'S FAR TOO YOUNG!

TWO ROYAL SUBJECTS.
BRONCO WILL EAT HIM ALIVE!

A ROYAL SUBJECT.
WHAT A PUNK!

A ROYAL SUBJECT.
HE'S GOT NO SHOT!

A ROYAL SUBJECT.
HE'LL NEVER SURVIVE!

DUKE FREDERICK. *(To* **CELIA** *and* **ROSALIND.***)* Speak to him ladies, see if you can move him.

CELIA. Young gentleman, we pray you for your own sake to embrace your safety and give over this attempt!

ROSALIND. Do, young sir!

ORLANDO. *(Not looking at* **ROSALIND** *and* **CELIA.***)* Let your gentle wishes go with me to my trial, wherein if I be foiled, there is but one shamed that was never gracious. I shall do the world no injury, for in it I have nothing.

ROSALIND. The little strength that I have, I would it were with you.

BRONCO. *(Mocking him in Spanish.)* ¿Tú eres Orlando? ¡Te voy a destruir! [Are you Orlando? I will destroy you!]

ORLANDO. Ready, sir!

DUKE FREDERICK. You shall try but one fall!

ALL.
THREE! TWO! ONE! FIGHT!

*(***BRONCO** *and* **ORLANDO** *wrestle!)*

UH-OH, UH-OH!
UH-OH, UH-OH!
DO YOU THINK HE CAN?

UH-OH, UH-OH!
UH-OH, UH-OH!
CAN HE? YES HE CAN!
WHAT AN UPSET!
WHO'DA THUNK IT?

ROSALIND.
OH, EXCELLENT YOUNG MAN!

ALL.
WHAT? NO! DAMN! WHOA!

(**ORLANDO** *pins* **BRONCO** *down.*)

REFEREE. One, two, three!

ANNOUNCER. And the winner's Orlando!

ALL.
ORLANDO, LANDO, HE'S THE MAN!
NO ONE CAN DO IT LIKE 'LANDO CAN!
ORLANDO, LANDO, HE'S THE MAN!
NO ONE CAN DO IT LIKE 'LANDO CAN!
ORLANDO, ORLANDO, ORLANDO!

DUKE FREDERICK. Who is thy father, young man?

(**ORLANDO** *removes his mask.*)

ORLANDO. My liege, I am the youngest son of Sir Rowland
de Boys.

[MUSIC 05 – AFTER THE MATCH]

DUKE FREDERICK. The son of Sir Rowland de Boys?
The world esteemed thy father honorable,
But I did find him still mine enemy.
Thou shouldst have better pleased me with this deed
hadst thou been son to some man else.

(**DUKE FREDERICK** *exits in a huff with his*
ROYAL MINIONS.)

(*The* **ROYAL SUBJECTS** *file out of the arena
hurriedly, wanting to escape the Duke's
wrath, leaving behind only* **ORLANDO,**
ROSALIND, CELIA, *and* **TOUCHSTONE.**)

ORLANDO. *(Aside.)*
I'M PROUD TO BE THE SON OF SIR ROWLAND DE BOYS!
AND I WOULDN'T TRADE THAT FOR A THING!
LET ALONE TO WIN THE FAVOR
OF SOME IRON-HANDED KING!

ROSALIND. *(Aside.)*
MY FATHER LOVED SIR ROWLAND DE BOYS,
AND IF HE WAS LIKE HIS SON, I CAN SEE WHY.

THIS GUY HAD NOTHING LEFT TO LOSE,
SO HE WENT FOR WHAT HE WANTED WITHOUT SHAME.
HE WOULDN'T PLAY THEIR GAME.

*(**ROSALIND** approaches **ORLANDO**.)*

ORLANDO,
I JUST WANTED YOU TO KNOW:
YOU INSPIRED ME TONIGHT.
AND I HAVEN'T MUCH TO GIVE,
BUT I WANT YOU TO HAVE THIS.
IT BELONGED TO MY DAD.
YOU DESERVE SOMETHING
FOR THE COURAGE THAT YOU HAD.

*(**ROSALIND** takes a chain off her neck and puts it around **ORLANDO**'s neck. He is speechless.)*

ORLANDO. ...

CELIA. Shall we go, coz?

ROSALIND. Fare you well.

*(**ROSALIND** starts to walk away from **ORLANDO**.)*

ORLANDO. *(Aside.)*
ORLANDO, STUPID ORLANDO!

ROSALIND.
IS HE STILL LOOKING MY WAY?

ORLANDO.
COULD YOU NOT EVEN SAY "THANKS"?

ROSALIND.
WHAT WAS HE TRYING TO SAY?

ORLANDO.
OR MAKE A SOUND?

ROSALIND.
WAIT, DID HE MAKE A SOUND?

ORLANDO.
YOUR BETTER PARTS ARE ALL THROWN DOWN!

ROSALIND.
SHOULD I TURN AROUND?

(**ROSALIND** *turns back.*)

ROSALIND. Did you call, sir?

ORLANDO. Hm?

ROSALIND. You wrestled well and conquered more than just your enemies.

ORLANDO. …

CELIA. Will you go, Rosalind?

TOUCHSTONE. Rosalind!

(**CELIA** *and* **TOUCHSTONE** *drag* **ROSALIND** *away, leaving* **ORLANDO** *alone.*)

ORLANDO.
SHE…
WHAT'S HAPPENING TO ME?
YOU…
WHAT ARE YOU SUPPOSED TO DO?
WHAT ARE YOU SUPPOSED TO, SUPPOSED TO DO?

(Enter one of Duke Frederick's **ROYAL MINIONS.***)*

ROYAL MINION. Good sir, I do in friendship counsel you
to leave this place.
Such is now the Duke's condition
That he misconstrues all that you have done.

ORLANDO. I thank you, friend.

*(***ROYAL MINION** *exits.)*

Thus must I from the smoke into the smother, from
tyrant duke unto a tyrant brother.

BUT – ROSALIND
ROSALIND!

(He exits.)

End of Scene

Scene Five
Rosalind's Dressing Chamber

(Enter **CELIA** *and* **ROSALIND**. *She hums to herself, picking up where Orlando's melody left off.)*

ROSALIND.
OOH... OOH OOH OOH

CELIA. Why, Rosalind! Cupid have mercy, not a word?

ROSALIND. Not one to throw at a dog.

CELIA. But is all this for your father?

ROSALIND. No, some of it is for my child's father!

CELIA. Is it possible on such a sudden you should fall into so strong a liking with old Sir Rowland's youngest son?

*(***DUKE FREDERICK*** enters with his* **ROYAL MINIONS**.*)*

[MUSIC 05A – ALL HAIL DUKE FREDERICK]

ROYAL MINIONS.
AH AH AH
ALL HAIL DUKE FRED'RICK!
AH AH AH
ALL HAIL DUKE FRED'RICK!

DUKE FREDERICK. *(To* **ROSALIND**.*)* Mistress, dispatch you with your safest haste, and get you from our court, or in the greatness of my word, you die.

ROSALIND. Me, uncle?

DUKE FREDERICK. You, niece.

ROSALIND. I do beseech your Grace,
Let me the knowledge of my fault bear with me.
Never so much as in a thought unborn

Did I offend your Highness!

DUKE FREDERICK. Thou art thy father's daughter. There's
enough.

ROSALIND. Treason is not inherited, my lord.
But my father was no traitor.
Then, good my liege, mistake me not so much to think
my poverty is treacherous!

CELIA. If she be a traitor, why, so am I!

DUKE FREDERICK. Ay, Celia, we stayed her for your sake,
Else had she with her father ranged along.
She is too subtle for thee, and her smoothness,
Her very silence and her patience speak to the people
and they pity her.
Thou wilt show more bright and seem more virtuous
when she is gone.
Firm and irrevocable is my doom.
She is banished!

ROYAL MINIONS.
AH AH AH
ALL HAIL DUKE FRED'RICK!
AH AH AH
ALL HAIL DUKE FRED'RICK!

(DUKE FREDERICK and ROYAL MINIONS exit.)

CELIA. O my poor Rosalind, whither wilt thou go?
Wilt thou change fathers? I will give thee mine.
I charge thee, be not thou more grieved than I am!

ROSALIND. I have more cause.

CELIA. Thou hast not, cousin.
Know'st thou not the duke
Hath banished me, his daughter?

ROSALIND. That he hath not.

CELIA. No, hath not? Rosalind lacks then the love
Which teacheth thee that thou and I am one.
Therefore devise with me how we may fly!

ROSALIND. Why, whither shall we go?

CELIA. To seek my uncle and his followers in the Forest of
Arden!

ROSALIND. Alas, what danger will it be to us to travel forth
so far? Beauty provoketh thieves sooner than gold.

CELIA. I'll put myself in poor and mean attire,
And with a kind of umber smirch my face.

ROSALIND. Were it not better,
Since I am more than common strong,
That I did suit me all points like a man?

CELIA. What shall I call thee when thou art a man?

ROSALIND. I'll have no worse a name than Jove's own page,
And therefore look you call me Ganymede!
But what will you be called?

CELIA. Something that hath a reference to my state:
No longer Celia, but Aliena.

ROSALIND. But, cousin, what if we assayed to steal
The clownish fool, Touchstone, out of your father's court?

CELIA. Leave me alone to woo him. Now go we in content
to liberty, and not to banishment!

(They exit.)

**[MUSIC 05B – TO LIBERTY AND NOT TO
BANISHMENT]**

End of Scene

Scene Six
The De Boys Estate

(**ORLANDO** *approaches his house, but is stopped by* **ADAM** *at the front gate.*)

ADAM. O unhappy youth, come not within these doors!
Your brother this night means to burn the lodging where you used to lie,
And you within it!

ORLANDO. Why, whither, Adam, wouldst thou have me go?
I rather will subject me to the malice of a diverted and bloody brother!

ADAM. But do not so!
I have five hundred crowns,
All this I give you. Let me be your servant.

ORLANDO. O good old man, come thy ways.

ADAM. I will follow thee to the last gasp with truth and loyalty.

ORLANDO. We'll go along together – to Arden!

[MUSIC 06 – IN ARDEN]

(*As* **ORLANDO** *and* **ROSALIND** *separately flee to the forest, the world of Arden spills forth onto the stage as drums in the distance grow closer and closer.*)

(*The* **PUPPET-DEERS** *enter. They prance and then are scared off as...*)

(*A community of* **ARDENITES** *enter, some playing drums.*)

(*They are led by* **DUKE SENIOR,** *who is accompanied by his posse of* **ATTENDANTS.**)

*(**JAQUES** follows and watches off to the side, scribbling in her notepad.)*

ALL.
IN ARDEN, OH IN ARDEN, OH IN ARDEN
HOW SHALL WE LEARN TO BE?

LOWER VOICES.
HOW SHALL WE LEARN TO BE?

HIGHER VOICES.
IN ARDEN,

ALL.
OH IN ARDEN, OH IN ARDEN
HOW SHALL WE LEARN TO BE?

LOWER VOICES.
HOW SHALL WE LEARN TO BE?

HIGHER VOICES.
IN ARDEN,

ALL.
OH IN ARDEN, OH IN ARDEN
HOW SHALL WE LEARN TO BE?

LOWER VOICES.
HOW SHALL WE LEARN TO BE?

HIGHER VOICES.
IN ARDEN,

ALL.
OH IN ARDEN, OH IN ARDEN
HOW SHALL WE LEARN TO BE?

LOWER VOICES.
HOW SHALL WE LEARN TO BE?

DUKE SENIOR.
CALLING ALL OUR FRIENDS AND FAMILY IN EXILE.
GATHER 'ROUND AS WE MAKE A SONG!

HOW SHALL WE SING OF GRACE IN THIS STRANGE PLACE?
I DON'T KNOW, BUT I'LL SING ALONG.

ALL.

IN ARDEN,

DUKE SENIOR.

WE SHALL TRY TO FIND THE USE OF OUR DISTRESS.

ALL.

IN ARDEN,

DUKE SENIOR.

WE SHALL ANSWER TO ADVERSITY WITH KINDNESS.

ALL.

IN ARDEN,

DUKE SENIOR.

WE SHALL SEEK THE BLESSINGS IN OUR MISERIES.

ALL.

WE SHALL LEARN TO SEE THE FOREST FOR THE TREES.

DUKE SENIOR & ATTENDANTS.

OH WHEN THE ICY WINTER WIND BENUMBS MY BODY,
EVEN THOUGH I SHIVER, I AM STILL ALIVE.
I SMILE AND THANK THE WIND FOR ITS HONESTY,
REMINDING MY SKIN IT'S THICK ENOUGH TO SURVIVE.

ALL.

IN ARDEN,

DUKE SENIOR & ATTENDANTS.

WE SHALL STUDY ALL THE SERMONS IN THE STONES.

ALL.

IN ARDEN,

DUKE SENIOR & ATTENDANTS.

WE SHALL HEAR THE LANGUAGE
OF OUR HEARTS AND BONES.

ALL.
IN ARDEN,

DUKE SENIOR & ATTENDANTS.
WE SHALL READ THE BOOK
IN THE BROOK AND SACRED SPRING.
WE SHALL LISTEN FOR THE TRUTH IN EVERYTHING.

ALL.
THE CAVE BECOMES OUR ROOF.
THE FIRE BECOMES OUR HEAT.
THE RAIN BECOMES OUR DRINK.
THE DEER BECOME OUR FOOD TO EAT!

JAQUES.
DO YOU REALIZE THAT THE DEER WE EAT FOR DINNER
ARE ACTUALLY THINKING, FEELING CREATURES
WHO LIVED HERE LONG BEFORE WE CAME?
AND WHEN WE OCCUPY THEIR NATIVE HOME
AND HUNT THEM DOWN,
WE'RE NO BETTER THAN YOUR BROTHER,
WHO DISPLACED US JUST THE SAME!

DUKE SENIOR. Oh Jaques. It does irk me – the poor dappled fools, should in their own confines have their round haunches gored.

JAQUES.
BUT THE DEER THEMSELVES ARE JUST AS BAD AS WE ARE!
I RECENTLY SAW ONE WITH AN ARROW IN HIS HEART,
ON HIS DYING BREATH,
AND WHEN THE OTHER DEER WENT BY,
THEY JUST IGNORED THEIR WOUNDED KIN.
DELIBERATELY LEAVING HER
TO A COLD AND LONELY DEATH!
AND ANOTHER THING:
WAIT, I LOST MY TRAIN OF THOUGHT...

DUKE SENIOR. Jaques, I love to cope with you in these sullen fits, for you are full of matter!

Everybody!

TWO, THREE, FOUR!

ALL.

IN ARDEN

DUKE SENIOR.

WE SHALL FIND OUT WHAT WE'RE MADE OF
FROM THE RAIN.

ALL.

IN ARDEN

JAQUES.

WE SHALL FIND WE'RE MADE OF SELFISHNESS AND PAIN!

ALL.

IN ARDEN

DUKE SENIOR.

WE SHALL SEARCH FOR HARMONY IN EV'RY TURN.

JAQUES.

WE SHALL MAKE THE SAME MISTAKES
AND NEVER LEARN!

DUKE SENIOR. Fie on thee, Jaques!

ALL.

IN ARDEN

DUKE SENIOR.

WE SHALL UNIFY!

ALL.

IN ARDEN

JAQUES.

WE SHALL ALL SOON DIE!

ALL.

IN ARDEN

DUKE SENIOR.

WE SHALL PITCH A TENT!

JAQUES.

WE SHALL RUIN THE ENVIRONMENT!

ALL.

IN ARDEN,
WE SHALL REACH OUT IN THE DARKNESS
AND ARISE!
IN ARDEN,
WE SHALL SEE THE LIGHT
WITHIN EACH OTHER'S EYES!
IN ARDEN,
WE SHALL MAKE A SANCTUARY ALL AS ONE!

DUKE SENIOR.

OUR LOVE SHALL BE OUR SHEPHERD AND OUR SUN!

JAQUES.

TIL IT BURNS OUT AND KILLS US ALL.

ALL.

TOGETHER WE'LL HEAL OUR WOUND.
TOGETHER WE'LL HEAL OUR

HIGHER VOICES.

WOUND.

LOWER VOICES.

TOGETHER WE'LL HEAL.

HIGHER VOICES.

TOGETHER WE'LL

ALL.

HEAL OUR WOUND,
TOGETHER WE'LL HEAL OUR WOUND
IN ARDEN!

[MUSIC 06A – IN ARDEN PLAYOFF]

(**DUKE SENIOR**, **JAQUES**, **ARDENITES**, **ATTENDANTS**, *and* **PUPPET-DEERS** *exit.)*

(**ROSALIND**, *now disguised as a young man named Ganymede, enters.)*

(**TOUCHSTONE** *enters, assisting a weary* **CELIA**, *now disguised as Aliena.)*

ROSALIND. Well, this is the Forest of Arden!

CELIA. O Jupiter, how weary are my spirits!

TOUCHSTONE. I care not for my spirits, if my legs were not weary.

ROSALIND. Courage, good Aliena.

CELIA. I cannot go no further, Touchstone.

TOUCHSTONE. Ay, now am I in Arden, the more fool I.

(*Enter* **PAPA CORIN** *and* **MAMA CORIN**, *a married pair of Ardenite farmers, with* **SILVIA**, *an Ardenite shepherdess.)*

Look you who comes here, a young woman and an old couple in solemn talk.

PAPA CORIN. That is the way to make her scorn you still, Silvia!

SILVIA. O Corin, that thou knew'st how I do love her!

MAMA CORIN. I partly guess, for I have loved ere now.

SILVIA. O, thou didst then never love so heartily.
If thou rememb'rest not the slightest folly
That ever love did make thee run into,
Thou hast not loved.

(**PHOEBE**, *another Ardenite shepherdess, walks by.)*

SILVIA. Or if thou hast not broke from company
    Abruptly, as my passion now makes me,
    Thou hast not loved!
    O Phoebe, Phoebe, Phoebe!

PHOEBE. Ugh!

      (**SILVIA** *runs off after* **PHOEBE**.)

ROSALIND. Alas, poor shepherd, searching of thy wound,
    I have by hard adventure found mine own.

CELIA. I pray you, one of you question yond pair, if they
    for gold will give us any food!

TOUCHSTONE. *(To* **MAMA** *and* **PAPA CORIN**.*)* Holla, you
    clowns!

ROSALIND. Peace, Touchstone! They are not thy kinsmen.

    (To **MAMA** *and* **PAPA CORIN**.*)* Good even to you, friends.

MAMA & PAPA CORIN. *(Together.)* And to you all.

ROSALIND. I prithee, shepherds, if that love or gold
    Can in this desert place buy entertainment,
    Bring us where we may rest ourselves and feed.
    Here's a young maid with travel much oppressed,
    And faints for succor.

MAMA CORIN. Fair sir, I pity her.
    But our cottage is now on sale,

PAPA CORIN. And at our sheepcote now, there is nothing
    That you will feed on.

MAMA CORIN. But what is, come see,
    And in my voice most welcome shall you be.

ROSALIND. I pray thee, if it stand with honesty,
    Buy thou the cottage,
    And thou shalt have to pay for it of us.

CELIA. And we will mend thy wages. I like this place,
And willingly could waste my time in it.

PAPA CORIN. We will your very faithful feeders be.

MAMA CORIN. And buy it with your gold right suddenly.

[MUSIC 06B – IN ARDEN PLAYOFF 2: RIGHT SUDDENLY]

(**MAMA** *and* **PAPA CORIN** *head off together.*)

(**ANDY**, *an Ardenite farmhand, walks by.*)

(**ANDY** *catches* **TOUCHSTONE**'s *eye.*)

ANDY. Good even, friend.

TOUCHSTONE. Good even.

(**TOUCHSTONE** *turns around and follows* **ANDY**.)

(*Enter* **ORLANDO** *and a weary* **ADAM**, *elsewhere in the forest.*)

ADAM. Dear master, I can go no further. O, I die for food! Here lie I down and measure out my grave.

ORLANDO. Hold death awhile at the arm's end, Adam. Come, I will bear thee to some shelter, and thou shalt not die for lack of a dinner, if there live anything in this desert!

(*They exit.*)

End of Scene

Scene Eight
The Feast

(The community of **ARDENITES** *enter with food, making preparations for the upcoming feast; An outdoor potluck picnic unfolds on stage.)*

[MUSIC 07 – UNDER THE GREENWOOD TREE]

AN ATTENDANT. I'll go seek Duke Senior. His banquet will be ready soon.

He hath been all this day to look for you, Jaques.

JAQUES. And I have been all this day to avoid him. He is too disputable for my company.

*(***DUKE SENIOR*** enters.)*

DUKE SENIOR. Why, how now, Jaques? What a world is this that your poor friends must woo your company?

JAQUES. A miserable world.

*(***DUKE SENIOR*** and ***JAQUES*** sit down with the* ***ARDENITES*** *at the picnic. The feast is ready. This song is their blessing before the meal.)*

ARDENITES.
SHA LA LA LA LA
SHA LA LA LA LA

DUKE SENIOR.
UNDER THE GREENWOOD TREE,
COME AND LIVE WITH ME
IF YOU WANNA BE FREE
UNDER THE GREENWOOD TREE,

ALL.
UNDER THE GREENWOOD TREE,

DUKE SENIOR.
I WILL NOT BE FREE
UNTIL WE ARE ALL FREE
UNDER THE GREENWOOD TREE,

ALL.
UNDER THE GREENWOOD TREE

DUKE SENIOR.
YOU SHALL SEE NO ENEMY,
YOU SHALL SEE NO ENEMY,
YOU SHALL SEE NO ENEMY.
DO NOT FEAR.

ALL.
ALL ARE WELCOME HERE.

DUKE SENIOR.
DO NOT FEAR.

ALL.
ALL ARE WELCOME HE–

(Enter **ORLANDO**, *brandishing a sword, interrupting the song.)*

ORLANDO. Forbear, and eat no more!
He dies that touches any of this fruit till I and my affairs are answered!
Forbear, I say!

DUKE SENIOR. What would you have? Your gentleness shall force
More than your force move us to gentleness.

ORLANDO. I almost die for food, and let me have it!

DUKE SENIOR. Sit down and feed, and welcome to our table.

ARDENITES. *(Simultaneously.)* Yeah, welcome! / Come on, sit down. / Grab a plate!

ORLANDO. Speak you so gently? Pardon me, I pray you.
I thought that all things had been savage here.
If ever you have looked on better days,
And know what 'tis to pity and be pitied,
Let gentleness my strong enforcement be,
In the which hope I blush and hide my sword.

DUKE SENIOR. True is it that we have seen better days.
Sit you down in gentleness.

ORLANDO. There is an old poor man
Who after me hath many a weary step
Limped in pure love. Till he be first sufficed,
I will not touch a bit.

DUKE SENIOR. Go find him out.

ORLANDO. I thank you; and be blessed for your good comfort.

(**ORLANDO** *exits.*)

DUKE SENIOR. Thou seest we are not all alone unhappy.
This wide and universal theater
Presents more woeful pageants than the scene
Wherein we play in.
Everybody sing!

(**ORLANDO** *comes back, carrying* **ADAM.**
Several **ARDENITES** *get up to assist them and
welcome them to the picnic.*)

ALL.
UNDER THE GREENWOOD
    TREE,
COME AND LIVE WITH ME
IF YOU WANNA BE FREE

UNDER THE GREENWOOD
    TREE,

DUKE SENIOR.

I SEE YOU AND YOU SEE ME.

COME BE

ALL.
> UNDER THE GREENWOOD TREE,
> YOU SHALL SEE NO ENEMY,
> YOU SHALL SEE NO ENEMY,
> YOU SHALL SEE NO ENEMY.
> DO NOT FEAR.
> ALL ARE WELCOME HERE.
> DO NOT FEAR.
> ALL ARE WELCOME HERE.

DUKE SENIOR.
> UNDER THE GREENWOOD TREE,

ARDENITES.
> SHA LA LA LA LA

DUKE SENIOR.
> UNDER THE GREENWOOD TREE,

ARDENITES.
> SHA LA LA LA LA

> (**DUKE SENIOR** *and* **ORLANDO** *step off to the side and have a hushed conversation, as the* **ARDENITES** *exit.*)

DUKE SENIOR. If that you were the good Sir Rowland's son,
> As you have whispered faithfully you were,
> Be truly welcome hither. I am the duke that loved your father.
> Give me your hand, and let me all your fortunes understand.

> (**DUKE SENIOR** *and* **ORLANDO** *exit.*)

End of Scene

Scene Nine
Meanwhile, Back in the Court

(**DUKE FREDERICK** *on his throne, surrounded by his* **ROYAL MINIONS** *and* **HISPERIA***.*)

[MUSIC 07A – ALL HAIL 2]

ROYAL MINIONS.
> AH AH AH
> ALL HAIL DUKE FRED'RICK!
> AH AH AH
> ALL HAIL DUKE FRED'RICK!

DUKE FREDERICK. Can it be possible that no man saw them? It cannot be!

A ROYAL MINION. My lord, the roinish clown Touchstone is also missing.

A ROYAL MINION. The Princess' gentlewoman, Hisperia, my liege.

HISPERIA. I confess that I secretly overheard
> Your daughter and her cousin much commend
> The parts and graces of Orlando, the wrestler!
> And I believe wherever they are gone
> That youth is surely in their company!

DUKE FREDERICK. Fetch Orlando hither.
> If he be absent, bring his brother Oliver to me.
> I'll make him find him.
> Do this suddenly, and let not search and inquisition quail
> To bring again these foolish runaways!

ROYAL MINIONS. Yes, your Dukeness!
> AH AH AH
> ALL HAIL DUKE FRED'RICK!

AH AH AH
ALL HAIL DUKE FRED'RICK!

(All exit.)

End of Scene

Scene Ten
Back in Arden

(Paper love notes are posted all over the trees. **ROSALIND** *enters, with one of them in her hand, reading it.* **CELIA** *and* **TOUCHSTONE** *read over her shoulder. He bursts out laughing.)*

TOUCHSTONE. Hahaha!

ROSALIND. Peace!

TOUCHSTONE. This is the very false gallop of verses. Why do you infect yourself with them?

ROSALIND. Peace, you dull fool. I found them on a tree.

TOUCHSTONE. Truly, the tree yields bad fruit.

*(***ORLANDO*** enters in a reverie. This song takes us inside his mind as he composes the love notes. He is accompanied by an imaginary boy band of ensemble dancers known as* **DE BOYS DANCERS.***)*

[MUSIC 08 – WILL U BE MY BRIDE]

ORLANDO. Rosalind, I'm carving your name on every tree
'Cause my love for you is like a seed
That blossoms into the flower of my soul
And that flower is watered by your beauty
And that water makes the pollen of my devotion even sweeter
For the bees of our hearts
I guess what I'm really trying to say is:

FROM THE MOMENT I SAW YOU, I KNEW.
ALL IT TOOK WAS JUST ONE SECOND TO KNOW
I WANNA MARRY YOU.

YOU'RE THE MOST PURE AND PERFECT GODDESS
HEAVEN COULD BRING.
I WOULDN'T CHANGE A SINGLE THING.
I JUST CAN'T WAIT TO ASK YOUR FATHER
FOR HIS BLESSING

DE BOYS DANCERS.

HIS BLESSING

ORLANDO.

THEN BUY YOU AN ANGEL WHITE DRESS.
THEN BABY, I'M HOPIN' YOU'LL SAY YES.

WILL U BE MY BRIDE?
I'LL LOVE YOU FOR ALL TIME
PLEASE MAKE ME THE LUCKIEST MAN ALIVE.
WILL U BE MY BRIDE?
I'LL KEEP YOU SAFE FOR LIFE.
WE'LL BE HAPPY EVER AFTER,

JUST JOY AND LAUGHTER.
WHEN WE RUN OFF IN THE SUNSET,
SINGING OUR LOVE SONG,
AS LONG AS WE'RE TOGETHER,
NOTHING WILL GO WRONG.
GIRL, I NEED YOUR PERFECT SMILE BY MY SIDE.
SO WILL U BE MY BRIDE?
WHOA
WILL U BE MY BRIDE?
OH YEAH, YEAH, YEAH, YEAH, YEAH.

GIRL, I WANNA SEE YOUR NAME WRITTEN NEXT TO MINE.
BUT FIRST I GOTTA THINK OF THE PERFECT RHYME.
YOU GIVE MY LIPS A PERMANENT GRIN.
I'D NEVER BE SAD WITH YOU, ROSALIND.
I WANNA WORSHIP ALL DAY AT YOUR SHRINE,
AT THE PEDESTAL OF MY ROSALINE –
WAIT, IS IT ROSALIND?
OR ROSALINE?
EITHER WAY, GIRL PLEASE BE MINE!

TOUCHSTONE. I'll rhyme you so eight years together. Let the forest judge!

> GIRL, YOU GOT NO FLAWS OR SIN.
> ARE YOU A DOLL OR A PERSON, ROSALIND?
> NO YOU'LL NEVER AGE OR START MENOPAUSALIN'
> 'CAUSE YOU'RE FOREVER TWENTY-ONE TO ME, ROSALIND.
> LET'S TIE THE KNOT SO I CAN GET THESE PAWS OF MINE
> ON THE SLENDER JAW OF ROSALINE! WHAT!
> 'CAUSE YOU KNEW I WAS TROUBLE WHEN I WALKED IN
> NEXT MISTAKE, MEET ROSALIND!

ROSALIND. Peace! Stand aside!

ORLANDO.

Girl, I feel like I confused you earlier with that flower metaphor.

So let me put it a different way.

My love for you is like –

A hamburger.

Rare, but also well-done.

But it's nothing without the bun of your affection,

And the onion rings on our fingers,

And a side of tater tots,

Like the tots we'll raise together.

But no pickles.

Pickles gross me out.

> WILL U BE MY BRIDE?
> I'LL LOVE YOU FOR ALL TIME
> PLEASE MAKE ME THE LUCKIEST MAN ALIVE.
> WILL U BE MY BRIDE?
> I'LL KEEP YOU SAFE FOR LIFE
> WE'LL BE HAPPY EVER AFTER,
> JUST JOY AND LAUGHTER.
> I WILL DIE WITHOUT YOUR SMILE BY MY SIDE.
> SO WILL U BE MY BRIDE?

WOAH?
WILL U BE MY BRIDE?
OH, I'M DOWN ON ONE KNEE
BEGGING YOU PLEASE
WILL U BE MY BRIDE?
OH YEAH, YEAH, YEAH, YEAH, YEAH.
WILL U BE MY BRIDE?

DE BOYS DANCERS.
BRIDE? BRIDE? BRIDE?

> (**ORLANDO** *and* **DE BOYS DANCERS** *disappear in a puff of smoke.*)

ROSALIND. O most gentle Jupiter. What a tedious homily of love.

CELIA. Touchstone, go off a little.

TOUCHSTONE. I will make an honorable retreat.

> (**TOUCHSTONE** *exits as he sings in a mocking tone.*)

"Will U be my bride, I'll love you for all tiiiime..."

CELIA. Didst thou hear these verses?

ROSALIND. O yes, I heard them all, and more too.

CELIA. But didst thou hear without wondering how thy name should be hanged and carved upon these trees?

ROSALIND. Is it a man?

CELIA. And a chain, that you once wore, about his neck.

ROSALIND. Orlando?

CELIA. Orlando.

ROSALIND. But doth he know that I am in this forest and in man's apparel?

> (*Enter* **ORLANDO**.)

CELIA. Soft, comes he not here?

ROSALIND. 'Tis he. Slink by, and note him.

  (**ROSALIND** *and* **CELIA** *step aside and hide.*
  JAQUES *enters.*)

JAQUES. I pray you mar no more trees with writing love songs in their barks!

ORLANDO. I pray you mar no more of my verses with reading them ill-favoredly.

JAQUES. Rosalind is your love's name?

ORLANDO. Yes, just.

JAQUES. I do not like her name.

ORLANDO. There was no thought in pleasing you when she was christened.

JAQUES. You have a nimble wit. Will you sit down with me? And we two will rail against our mistress the world and all our misery.

ORLANDO. I will chide no breather in the world but myself, against whom I know most faults.

JAQUES. The worst fault you have is to be in love.

ORLANDO. 'Tis a fault I will not change for your best virtue. I am weary of you, Jaques.

JAQUES. I do desire we may be better strangers.

ORLANDO. Adieu, Miss Melancholy.

JAQUES. Farewell, Signior Love.

ROSALIND. *(Aside to* **CELIA.***)* I will speak to him like a saucy lackey, and under that habit play the knave with him.

(As Ganymede.) Do you hear, forester?

ORLANDO. Very well. What would you?

ROSALIND. *(As Ganymede.)* I pray you, what is't o'clock?

ORLANDO. You should ask me what time o' day. There's no clock in the forest.

ROSALIND. *(As Ganymede.)* Then there is no true lover in the forest; else sighing every minute and groaning every hour would detect the lazy foot of time as well as a clock.

ORLANDO. Where dwell you, pretty youth?

ROSALIND. *(As Ganymede.)* With this shepherdess, my sister, here in the skirts of the forest, like fringe upon a petticoat.

ORLANDO. Your accent is something finer than you could purchase in so removed a dwelling.

ROSALIND. *(As Ganymede.)* I have been told so of many. There is a man haunts the forest that abuses our young plants with carving "Rosalind" on their barks, hangs odes upon hawthorns and elegies on brambles, all, forsooth, deifying the name of Rosalind. If I could meet that fancy-monger, I would give him some good counsel, for he seems to have the quotidian of love upon him.

ORLANDO. I am he, that unfortunate he, that is so love-shaked.

ROSALIND. *(As Ganymede.)* There is none of my uncle's marks upon you. He taught me how to know a man in love, in which cage of rushes I am sure you are not prisoner.

ORLANDO. What were his marks?

ROSALIND. *(As Ganymede.)* A lean cheek, which you have not, an unquestionable spirit, which you have not; a beard neglected, which you have not. You are rather point-device in your accouterments, as loving yourself than seeming the lover of any other.

ORLANDO. Fair youth, I would I could make thee believe I love!

ROSALIND. *(As Ganymede.)* But are you so much in love as your rhymes speak?

ORLANDO. Neither rhyme nor reason can express how much.

ROSALIND. *(As Ganymede.)* Love is merely a madness. Yet, I profess curing it by counsel.

ORLANDO. I pray you tell me your remedy.

[MUSIC 09 – IMAGINE I'M YOUR LOVER]

ROSALIND.
IMAGINE I'M YOUR LOVER.
PRETEND TO WOO ME.
I'LL SHOW YOU HOW THE GIRL WOULD TRULY BE.
I'LL FLIRT WITH YOU ONE SECOND,
ACT LIKE I DON'T CARE THE NEXT.
DROP A BREADCRUMB I ADORE YOU,
THEN IGNORE YOUR TEXT.
STARE YOU DOWN, THEN LOOK AWAY.
MEAN SOMETHIN' DIFF'RENT THAN I SAY.
YEAH, I'LL CURE YOU OF YOUR HEARTACHE
TIL YOU RECOVER
IF YOU IMAGINE I'M YOUR LOVER.

ORLANDO. I would not be cured, youth.

ROSALIND. *(As Ganymede.)* I would cure you.

JUST IMAGINE I'M YOUR LOVER.
PRETEND TO WOO ME.
WHAT WOULD YOU SAY IF SHE WERE ME RIGHT NOW?

ORLANDO.
I'D SAY, "YOUR EYES ARE MAGIC!"

ROSALIND.
THAT WOULD MAKE ME DISAPPEAR.

ORLANDO.
I'D PROPOSE TO YOU WITH ROSES!

ROSALIND.
HOW 'BOUT WE START WITH A BEER?

ORLANDO.
I'D ASK TO MEET YOUR PARENTS FIRST!

ROSALIND.
I'M NOT A BABY TO BE NURSED!
BOY, YOU'LL LEARN WHAT LOVE IS REALLY LIKE
UNDER THE COVER
IF YOU IMAGINE I'M –

ORLANDO.
I'D RUN A THOUSAND MILES TO PROVE MY LOVE!

ROSALIND.
IN CIRCLES IN YOUR HEAD.

ORLANDO.
I'D SAVE YOU FROM THE MONSTERS!

ROSALIND.
AND I'D HIDE UNDER MY BED.

ORLANDO.
I'D MAKE ALL YOUR DREAMS COME TRUE.

ROSALIND.
WAIT, WHO TOLD MY DREAMS TO YOU?

ORLANDO.
I WANNA LEARN WHAT LOVE IS REALLY LIKE...

ROSALIND.
IF YOU IMAGINE!

ORLANDO.
IMAGINE?

ROSALIND.
IMAGINE...

ORLANDO.
IF I IMAGINE...

ROSALIND & ORLANDO.
IMAGINE,

ROSALIND.
IMAGINE I'M YOUR LOVER,
AND PRETEND TO WOO ME.

ORLANDO. Now by the faith of my love, I will, good youth.

ROSALIND. *(As Ganymede.)* Nay, you must call me Rosalind.

(They exit.)

End of Scene

Scene Eleven
Elsewhere in Arden

(**TOUCHSTONE** *and* **ANDY** *enter, in a flirtatious chase.*)

TOUCHSTONE. Good Andy! Am I the man yet? Doth my simple feature content you?

ANDY. Your features, Lord warrant us! What features?

TOUCHSTONE. Truly, I would the gods had made thee poetical.

ANDY. I do not know what "poetical" is. Is it honest in deed and word? Is it a true thing?

TOUCHSTONE. No, truly, for the truest poetry is the most feigning, and lovers are given to poetry, and what they swear in poetry may be said as lovers they do feign.

ANDY. Do you wish, then, that the gods had made me poetical?

TOUCHSTONE. I do, truly, for thou swear'st to me thou art honest. Now if thou wert a poet, I might have some hope thou didst feign.

ANDY. Would you not have me honest?

TOUCHSTONE. No, truly, unless thou wert hard-favored; for honesty coupled to beauty is to have honey a sauce to sugar.

ANDY. Well, I am not fair, and therefore I pray the gods make me honest.

TOUCHSTONE. Be it as it may be, I will marry thee, and to that end, I have been with Martext, the vicar of Arden, who hath promised to meet me in this place of the forest and to couple us!

ANDY. Well, the gods give us joy!

TOUCHSTONE. Amen. A man may, if he were of a fearful heart, stagger in this attempt, for here we have no temple but the wood. But what though? Courage! Here comes the vicar.

(**MARTEXT,** *an Ardenite priestess, enters.*)

Madam Martext, will you dispatch us here under this tree, or shall we go with you to your chapel?

MARTEXT. Is there none here to give the man?

TOUCHSTONE. I will not take him on gift of any man.

MARTEXT. Truly, he must be given, or the marriage is not lawful.

TOUCHSTONE. *(Pulling* **MARTEXT** *aside.)* I were better to be married by you than by another, for you are not like to marry me well, and not being well married, it will be a good excuse for me to leave my husband.

ANDY. *(He heard that.)* What!?

(**ANDY** *whacks* **TOUCHSTONE**, *offended, and storms off.*)

TOUCHSTONE. Andy! Sweet Andy!

(**TOUCHSTONE** *runs off after him.*)

End of Scene

Scene Twelve
Elsewhere in Arden

(**ROSALIND** *is pacing quickly.* **CELIA** *races to keep up with her.*)

ROSALIND. Why did he swear he would come this morning, and comes not?

CELIA. Nay, certainly, there is no truth in him.

ROSALIND. Not true in love?

CELIA. Yes, when he is in, but I think he is not in.

ROSALIND. You have heard him swear downright he was.

CELIA. "Was" is not "is." Besides, the oath of a lover is no stronger than the word of a tapster. They are both the confirmer of false reckonings. Orlando attends here in the forest on the duke your father.

ROSALIND. I met the duke yesterday and had much question with him. He asked me of what parentage I was. I told him, of as good as he. So he laughed and let me go. But what talk we of fathers when there is such a man as Orlando?

(**MAMA** *and* **PAPA CORIN** *enter.*)

MAMA CORIN. Aliena and Ganymede! You have oft inquired
After Silvia, the shepherd that complained of love,
Praising the proud disdainful Phoebe
That was her mistress.

CELIA. (*As Aliena.*) Well, and what of her?

PAPA CORIN. If you will see a pageant truly played, go hence a little!

ROSALIND. (*As Ganymede, to* **MAMA** *and* **PAPA CORIN.**)
Bring us to this sight,

[MUSIC 10 – YOU PHOEBE ME]

ROSALIND. and you shall say
I'll prove a busy actor in their play.

(They find a place to hide and watch as
PHOEBE *enters, followed by* **SILVIA**.*)*

SILVIA.
SWEET PHOEBE,
DON'T SNUB ME.
SAY THAT YOU LOVE ME NOT,
BUT MUST YOU BE THIS COLD?
YOUR DARK EYES THROW A DART
THROUGH THE BULLSEYE OF MY HEART.
YOU KNOW I WANT YOU SO.
CAN'T YOU JUST LET ME DOWN EASY?
'STEAD YOU SCORN ME.
YOU TAUNT ME.
YOU RIDICULE AND HAUNT ME.

YOU PHOEBE ME.
YOU PHOEBE ME.
YOU PHOEBE ME.
WHY YOU GOTTA PHOEBE ME?

YOU PHOEBE ME.
YOU PHOEBE ME.
WHY YOU GOTTA PHOEBE ME?

PHOEBE.
YOU SAY MY GLANCE IS LETHAL,
BUT GIRL, I KNOW YOU'RE LYING.
'CAUSE I'M GIVING YOU A DEATH STARE,

(**PHOEBE** *shoots* **SILVIA** *a death stare.)*

AND I DON'T SEE YOU DYING!

SILVIA.
LOVE INJURIES AREN'T THE KIND YOU CAN SEE BLEED.
IF ONLY YOU KNEW WHAT IT'S LIKE TO BE PHOEBE'D!

(**ROSALIND**, *as Ganymede, inserts herself into their argument.*)

ROSALIND.

SWEET PHOEBE,
EXCUSE ME.
YOU SHOULD BE THANKING GOD
FOR SENDING SUCH A CATCH.
YOU FOUND A GOOD SPOT, SO PARK IT.
SELL WHEN YOU CAN,
'CAUSE YOU'RE NOT FOR ALL MARKETS.

(*To* **SILVIA.**)

AND YOU, WHY DO YOU WANT HER SO?
SHE PHOEBES YOU.
SHE PHOEBES YOU.
SHE PHOEBES YOU.
DON'T YOU LET HER PHOEBE YOU.
YOU BETTER LOSE THE ROSE-COLORED LENS
YOU SEE HER THROUGH
DON'T YOU LET HER PHOEBE YOU.

PHOEBE.

SWEET YOUTH,
I'D RATHER HEAR YOU CHIDE
THAN THIS WOMAN WOO!

ROSALIND.

WHAT?
ME?
NO!
YOU SAY MY WORDS ARE TEMPTING,
BUT GIRL YOU'RE WAY OFF TRACK.
SO IF YOU TRY AND COURT ME,
I'MA PHOEBE YOU RIGHT BACK!
I PHOEBE YOU.

SILVIA. *(To* **ROSALIND**.*)*
YOU PHOEBE WHO?

ROSALIND. *(To* **SILVIA**.*)*
SHE PHOEBES YOU.

SILVIA.
WHY YOU GOTTA PHOEBE TOO?

ROSALIND. 'Tis such fools as you that makes the world full of ill-favored children!

(**ROSALIND** *storms off with* **CELIA** *and* **THE CORINS** *in tow.*)

PHOEBE.
SWEET FELLA
HE SNUBBED ME.
HE SAID HE LOVES ME NOT,
BUT MUST HE BE THIS COLD?
OH, I WANT HIM SO.
WHY DOES HIS DISREGARD PLEASE ME?
HE SCORNS ME.
HE TAUNTS ME.
HE RIDICULES AND HAUNTS ME.

SILVIA.
DON'T YOU SEE?
HE PHOEBES YOU.
HE PHOEBES YOU.
HE PHOE–

PHOEBE. *(Ignoring/interrupting* **SILVIA**.*)* I'll write to him a very taunting letter, and thou shalt bear it. Wilt thou, Silvia?

SILVIA. Phoebe, with all my heart.

(**PHOEBE** *exits, leaving* **SILVIA** *alone.*)

YOU PHOEBE ME.
YOU PHOEBE ME.
YOU PHOEBE ME.
WHY YOU GOTTA PHOEBE ME LIKE YOU DO?
I WISH YOU'D PHOEBE ME
THE WAY I PHOEBE YOU.

(**SILVIA** *exits.*)

End of Scene

Scene Thirteen
A Hootenanny in Arden

[MUSIC 10A – THE DEER HUNT]

(The **PUPPET-DEERS** *enter chased by* **HUNTERS.**
The **PUPPET-DEERS** *scatter away.)*

JAQUES. Sweep on, you fat and greasy citizens! 'Tis just the fashion!

> *(***DUKE SENIOR*** *enters, with his* **ATTENDANTS** *and* **ARDENITES** *in tow, gathering for a community dance party – a hootenanny!)*

DUKE SENIOR. Must you moralize this spectacle?

JAQUES. Give me leave to speak my mind, and I will through and through
Cleanse the infected world, if they will patiently receive my medicine!

DUKE SENIOR. I have a song for this purpose!

JAQUES. Of course you do.

DUKE SENIOR. And a dance!

[MUSIC 11 – OH DEER]

Come! Warble! Miss Amiens, shall we?

> *(***DUKE SENIOR*** *beckons more* **ARDENITES** *on stage for the hootenanny. The* **ARDENITES** *partner off for a social dance.)*

> *(***DUKE SENIOR, MISS AMIENS,*** *and the* **ATTENDANTS** *serenade them.)*

> *(Throughout the song, a dance love triangle ensues.* **ANDY** *is the life of the party – dancing with everyone, but ignoring* **TOUCHSTONE.***)*

(**WILLIAM**, *an attractive Ardenite, asks* **ANDY** *to dance.*)

(**TOUCHSTONE** *looks on, growing increasingly jealous.*)

(**TOUCHSTONE** *tries unsuccessfully to cut in and win* **ANDY** *back.*)

DUKE SENIOR & MISS AMIENS.
OH DEER, MY DEAR
MY DOSEY-DOE,
I'M WHITE-HOT ON YOUR TRAIL.
EVER SINCE YOU PRANCED MY WOODSY WAY,
BEEN WISHIN' WE COULD SHAKE A TAIL.

BUT DEER, MY DEAR,
MY DOSEY-DOE,
YOU'RE GIVING ME THE RUN-AROUND.
YOU CAN TRY TO THROW ME OFF YOUR SCENT,
BUT SOON I'M GONNA HUNT YOU DOWN.
I'M GONNA HUNT YOU DOWN.

ATTENDANTS.
GONNA HUNT YOU DOWN!

DUKE SENIOR & MISS AMIENS.
GONNA HUNT YOU

ALL.
DOWN, DOWN, DOWN.

DUKE SENIOR & MISS AMIENS.
YOU MAY BE BIG GAME, DEARIE, BUT

ALL.
SOON I'M GONNA HUNT YOU DOWN.
(*Dance break!*)

BACK IN THE CITY,
I WAS SO STUCK IN MY PETTY PACE.

ALL.

I NEVER FOUND A HART LIKE YOU.
NOW I LIVE FOR THE THRILL OF THE CHASE.

DUKE SENIOR & MISS AMIENS.

SO DEER, MY DEAR,
MY LUCKY BUCK,
COME HOOF ALONG WITH ME.
OUR PARENTS' PARENTS DID THIS DANCE.
THE APPLE OUGHTA FALL BY THE TREE.
I'M GONNA HUNT YOU DOWN.

ATTENDANTS.

GONNA HUNT YOU DOWN!

DUKE SENIOR & MISS AMIENS.

GONNA HUNT YOU

ALL.

DOWN, DOWN, DOWN.

DUKE SENIOR & MISS AMIENS.

YOU MAY BE BIG GAME, DEARIE, BUT

ALL.

SOON I'M GONNA HUNT YOU DOWN.

DUKE SENIOR.

I WON'T GO STAG!

ALL.

YOU MAY BE BIG GAME, DEARIE,
BUT SOON I'M GONNA HUNT YOU DOWN.
WEE-HOO!

(All exit.)

End of Scene

Scene Fourteen
Elsewhere in Arden

[MUSIC 11A – OH DEER PLAYOFF/"ALL THE WORLD'S A STAGE"]

(As everyone else saunters off, **JAQUES** *is in her own little world, still working on her unfinished philosophy...)*

JAQUES.
ALL THE WORLD'S A STAGE,
ALL THE WORLD'S A STAGE...

(She struggles to come up with the next line. **ROSALIND** *and* **CELIA** *enter.)*

ROSALIND. *(As Ganymede.)* They say you are a melancholy person.

JAQUES. I do love it better than laughing.

ROSALIND. *(As Ganymede.)* Those that are in extremity of either are abominable fellows.

JAQUES. It is a melancholy of mine own, okay? And I'm trying to write something right now, so I'm not really in a social mood.

ROSALIND. *(As Ganymede.)* What has't thee writ so far?

JAQUES. Oh! Well, um, it's just a first draft and it's still pretty rough but it goes something like...

ALL THE WORLD'S A STAGE
AND EVERYBODY'S –

(Enter **ORLANDO,** *interrupting.)*

ORLANDO. Good day and happiness, dear Rosalind.

JAQUES. Oh look, it's Romeo's understudy.

ROSALIND. *(As Ganymede.)* Why, how now, Orlando, where have you been all this while?

ORLANDO. My fair Rosalind, I come within an hour of my promise.

ROSALIND. *(As Ganymede.)* Break an hour's promise in love?

ORLANDO. Pardon me –

ROSALIND. *(As Ganymede.)* Nay, an you be so tardy, come no more in my sight!

ORLANDO. My dear Rosalind!

ROSALIND. *(As Ganymede.)* Come, woo me, woo me, for now I am in a holiday humor, and like enough to consent. What would you say to me now if I were your very, very Rosalind?

ORLANDO. I would kiss before I spoke.

ROSALIND. *(As Ganymede.)* Nay, you were better speak first. Very good orators, when they are out, they will spit; and for lovers lacking the cleanliest shift is to kiss.

ORLANDO. How if the kiss be denied?

ROSALIND. *(As Ganymede.)* Then she puts you to entreaty, and there begins new matter.

ORLANDO. Who could be out, being before his beloved mistress?

ROSALIND. *(As Ganymede.)* Marry, that should you if I were your mistress, or I should think my honesty ranker than my wit.

ORLANDO. What, of my suit?

ROSALIND. *(As Ganymede.)* Not out of your apparel, and yet out of your suit. Am I not your Rosalind?

ORLANDO. I take some joy to say you are because I would be talking of her.

ROSALIND. *(As Ganymede.)* Well, in her person, I say I will not have you.

ORLANDO. Then, in mine own person I die.

ROSALIND. *(As Ganymede.)* No, faith, die by attorney. The poor world is almost six thousand years old, and in all this time there was not any man died in his own person in a love cause. These are all lies. Men have died from time to time and worms have eaten them, but not for love.

ORLANDO. I would not have my right Rosalind of this mind, for I protest her frown might kill me.

ROSALIND. *(As Ganymede.)* By this hand, it will not kill a fly. But come; now I will be your Rosalind in a more coming-on disposition, and ask me what you will, I will grant it.

ORLANDO. Then love me, Rosalind.

ROSALIND. *(As Ganymede.)* Yes, faith, will I, Fridays and Saturdays and all. – Come, sister, you shall be the priest and marry us. – Give me your hand, Orlando.

> *(****ROSALIND**** and **ORLANDO** take hands. It's the first time they've physically touched. A spark.)*

ORLANDO. *(To* **CELIA***.)* Pray thee marry us.

CELIA. *(As Aliena.)* I cannot say the words.

ROSALIND. *(As Ganymede.)* You must begin "Will you, Orlando –"

CELIA. *(As Aliena.)* Go to – Will you, Orlando, have to wife this Rosalind?

ORLANDO. I will.

ROSALIND. *(As Ganymede.)* Ay, but when?

ORLANDO. Why now, as fast as she can marry us.

ROSALIND. *(As Ganymede.)* Then you must say "I take thee, Rosalind, for wife."

ORLANDO. I take thee, Rosalind, for wife.

ROSALIND. *(As Ganymede.)* Now tell me how long you would have her after you have possessed her?

ORLANDO. Forever and a day.

ROSALIND. *(As Ganymede.)* Say "a day" without the "ever." No, no, Orlando, men are April when they woo, December when they wed. Maids are May when they are maids, but the sky changes when they are wives.

[MUSIC 12 – WHEN I'M YOUR WIFE]

I'LL START CRYING AT RANDOM WHILE WE'RE HAVING FUN,
AND DIE LAUGHING WHEN YOU'RE TRYING TO SLEEP.
I'LL BE JEALOUS OF ANYTHING PRIVATE OF YOURS,
BUT I'LL BURY MY OWN SECRETS DEEP.
I'LL FREQUENTLY SABOTAGE GENUINE MOMENTS
WITH MAKE-BELIEVE STRIFE.
I'LL FLUCTUATE BOTH FOR THE WORSE AND THE BETTER
WHEN I'M YOUR WIFE.

ORLANDO. But will my Rosalind do so?

ROSALIND. By my life, she will do as I do.

I WON'T BE THE UNBLEMISHED IDEAL
YOU'VE BEEN FOOLING YOURSELF TO BELIEVE THAT I AM.
I'LL BERATE YOU FOR DOUBTING MY POWER,
THEN SEEK REASSURANCE THAT I'M NOT A SHAM.
MY THIRST FOR CONTROL
AND MY PENCHANT FOR DRAMA
WILL LIKELY RUN RIFE.
I'LL PUBLISH NEW VERSIONS OF ME EVERY HOUR
WHEN I'M YOUR WIFE.

ORLANDO. O, but she is wise!

ROSALIND. Or else she could not have the wit to do this.

THE WISER THE WOMAN, THE WILDER SHE IS.
SO BEFORE IT'S TOO LATE, YOU SHOULD KNOW:
THE CLOSER YOU HOLD ME, THE FARTHER I'LL GO.

I WILL HARBOR RESENTMENTS I HAVE TOWARDS MY DAD,
AND UNFAIRLY PROJECT THEM ON YOU.
I'LL WONDER IF YOU'RE GONNA LEAVE ME LIKE HE DID,
NO MATTER HOW OFTEN YOU SAY IT'S NOT TRUE.
I'LL BLAME YOU FOR WOUNDS IN MY HEART
THAT WERE CAUSED BY ANOTHER MAN'S KNIFE.
IT MIGHT TAKE ME DECADES
TO SORT THROUGH THIS BAGGAGE
WHEN I'M YOUR WIFE.

I CAN'T PROMISE I'LL BE THE SAME PERSON
FIVE OR FIFTY YEARS FROM NOW,
SO I SUGGEST YOU DECIDE YOUR RESPONSE
BEFORE TAKING YOUR VOW.
DESPITE ALL OF THIS,
COULD YOU STILL LOVE ME
FOR WHAT'S LEFT OF MY LIFE
WHEN I'M YOUR WIFE?
WHEN I'M YOUR WIFE?

ORLANDO. I must attend the Duke at dinner. For these two hours, Rosalind, I will leave thee.

ROSALIND. *(As Ganymede.)* Ay, go your ways, go your ways. I knew what you would prove. If you come one minute behind your hour, I will think you the most hollow lover, and the most unworthy of her you call Rosalind. Therefore keep your promise.

ORLANDO. With no less religion than if thou wert indeed my Rosalind.

ROSALIND. *(As Ganymede.)* Adieu.

*(**ORLANDO** exits.)*

CELIA. We must have your doublet and hose plucked over your head and show the world what the bird hath done to her own nest!

ROSALIND. O coz, coz, coz, that thou didst know how many fathom deep I am in love.

(They exit.)

End of Scene

Scene Fifteen
Meanwhile, Back in the Court

(The **ROYAL MINIONS** *drag on* **OLIVER** *and present him to* **DUKE FREDERICK.***)*

[MUSIC 12A – ALL HAIL 3]

ROYAL MINIONS & ROYAL SUBJECTS.
AH AH AH
ALL HAIL DUKE FRED'RICK!
AH AH AH
ALL HAIL DUKE FRED'RICK!

A ROYAL MINION. We present Oliver de Boys, Your Dukeness!

A ROYAL MINION. He swears he has not seen his brother Orlando since the wrestling.

DUKE FREDERICK. *(To* **OLIVER.***)* Not seen him since? Sir, sir, that cannot be.
Find out thy brother wheresoe'er he is.
Bring him, dead or living,
Or thy lands do we seize into our hands.

OLIVER. O that your highness knew my heart in this.
I never loved my brother in my life.

DUKE FREDERICK. More villain thou. Well, push him out of doors, and turn him going to Arden!

(The **ROYAL MINIONS** *throw* **OLIVER** *out.)*

ROYAL MINIONS & ROYAL SUBJECTS.
AH AH AH
ALL HAIL DUKE FRED'RICK!
AH AH AH
ALL HAIL DUKE FRED'RICK!

(All exit.)
End of Scene

Scene Sixteen
Back in Arden

(Enter **ROSALIND** *and* **CELIA**. **SILVIA** *runs on, a letter in hand.)*

SILVIA. Ganymede! My gentle Phoebe did bid me give you this.
I know not the contents, but as I guess
It bears an angry tenor. Pardon me.
I am but as a guiltless messenger.

*(***ROSALIND*** reads the letter.)*

ROSALIND. *(As Ganymede.)* She says I am not fair, that I lack manners.
She calls me proud, and that she could not love me.
She Phoebes me!
This is a letter of your own device!

SILVIA. No, I protest! I know not the contents. Phoebe did write it.

CELIA. *(As Aliena.)* Alas, poor shepherd.

ROSALIND. *(As Ganymede.)* No, she deserves no pity. Wilt thou love such a woman? Say this to her: that if she love me, I charge her to love thee. If you be a true lover, hence, and not a word, for here comes more company.

*(***SILVIA*** exits.)*

(Enter **OLIVER**.*)*

OLIVER. Good morrow, fair ones. Pray you, if you know,
Where in the purlieus of this forest stands
A sheepcote fenced about with olive trees?

*(***CELIA*** turns around. She and* **OLIVER** *lock eyes. A spark.)*

[MUSIC 12B – CELIA MEETS OLIVER – AFTER THE MATCH THEME]

CELIA. *(As Aliena.)* West of this place, down in the neighbor bottom.

OLIVER. Are not you the owner of the house I did inquire for?

CELIA. *(As Aliena.)* It is no boast, being asked, to say we are.

OLIVER. …

CELIA. …

OLIVER. Orlando doth commend him to you both.

> *(***ROSALIND** *jumps in, breaking their spell, cutting off the music.)*

ROSALIND. *(As Ganymede.)* Orlando?

OLIVER. And to that youth he calls his Rosalind, he sends this bloody napkin. Are you he?

> *(He shows a bloodstained handkerchief.)*

ROSALIND. *(As Ganymede.)* I am. What must we understand by this?

OLIVER. Some of my shame, if you will know of me
What man I am, and how, and why, and where
This handkerchief was stained.

CELIA. *(As Aliena.)* I pray you tell it.

OLIVER. When last the young Orlando parted from you,
He left a promise to return again

Within an hour, and pacing through the forest,
Lo, what befell!

[MUSIC 13 – THE LION & THE SNAKE]

(As **OLIVER** *retells the story, the memory of it is theatricalized. For example, we used puppets!)*

*(***ORLANDO*** *enters, pacing through the forest.)*

OLIVER. Under an old oak,
A wretched, ragged man lay sleeping on his back.

(We see a man sleeping.)

About his neck, a green and gilded snake had wreathed itself,

(The snake wreathes itself around the man's neck.)

But suddenly, seeing Orlando, it did slip away into a bush!

(The snake slips away into a bush, as the lioness appears.)

Under which a lioness lay couching, with catlike watch.

(The lioness lurks.)

This seen, Orlando did approach the man

*(***ORLANDO*** *approaches the wretched, ragged, sleeping man.)*

And found it was his brother, his elder brother.

*(***CELIA*** *presses "pause" on the memory, freezing it – wait, wait, wait!)*

CELIA. *(As Aliena.)* O, I have heard him speak of that same brother,
And he did render him the most unnatural
That lived amongst men.

OLIVER. And well he might so do,
For well I know he was unnatural.

ROSALIND. *(As Ganymede.)* But to Orlando: did he leave him there,
Food to the sucked and hungry lioness?

(The memory and the music resume.)

OLIVER. Twice did he turn his back and purposed so,
But kindness, nobler ever than revenge,
Made him give battle to the lioness;

*(**ORLANDO** battles the lioness!)*

*(**ORLANDO** wins and the lioness runs away,
though **ORLANDO** has been hurt in the process.)*

In which hurtling, from miserable slumber I awaked.

*(As **OLIVER** inserts himself into the memory,
it dissolves away.)*

CELIA. *(As Aliena.)* Was't you he rescued?

ROSALIND. *(As Ganymede.)* Are you his brother that did so oft contrive to kill him?

OLIVER. T'was I, but 'tis not I.

ROSALIND. *(As Ganymede.)* But for the bloody napkin??

OLIVER. By and by,
When from the first to the last betwixt us two
Tears our recountments had most kindly bathed,
He stripped himself, and here upon his arm
The lioness had torn some flesh away,
And now he fainted, and cried in fainting upon Rosalind.
He sent me hither, stranger as I am,
To tell this story, that you might excuse
His broken promise.

*(**ROSALIND** faints.)*

CELIA. *(As Aliena.)* Why, how now, Ganymede, sweet Ganymede? Cousin Ganymede?

> *(***ROSALIND*** *regains consciousness, trying to play down her fainting.)*

ROSALIND. *(As Ganymede.)* I pray you tell your brother how well I counterfeited. Heigh-ho.

OLIVER. This was not counterfeit.

ROSALIND. *(As Ganymede.)* Counterfeit, I assure you.

CELIA. *(As Aliena.)* Pray you draw homewards. Good sir, go with us.

OLIVER. That will I, for I must bear answer back
How you excuse my brother, Rosalind.

ROSALIND. *(As Ganymede.)* I shall devise something. Will you go?

> *(All exit.)*

End of Scene

Scene Seventeen
Elsewhere in Arden

*(***TOUCHSTONE*** *and* **ANDY** *enter bickering.)*

TOUCHSTONE. We shall find a time, Andy! Patience, gentle Andy!

ANDY. Faith, that priest was good enough!

TOUCHSTONE. A most wicked Martext, Andy, a most vile vicar. But, Andy, there is a youth here in the forest lays claim to you.

ANDY. Ay, I know who 'tis. He hath no interest in me in the world. Here comes the man you mean.

*(***WILLIAM*** *enters. He smiles at* **ANDY**.*)*

WILLIAM. Good ev'n, Andy!

ANDY. Good ev'n, William.

TOUCHSTONE. Good even, gentle friend!

WILLIAM. And good ev'n to you, sir.

TOUCHSTONE. How old are you, friend?

WILLIAM. Five-and-twenty, sir.

TOUCHSTONE. A ripe age. Is thy name William?

WILLIAM. William, sir.

TOUCHSTONE. A fair name. You do love this man?

WILLIAM. I do, sir!

TOUCHSTONE. Art thou learned?

WILLIAM. No, sir.

TOUCHSTONE. Then learn this of me: to have is to have. For all your writers do consent that ipse is "he." Now, you are not ipse, for I am he.

WILLIAM. Which he, sir?

TOUCHSTONE.   He, sir, that must marry this man. Therefore, you clown, abandon – which is in the vulgar "leave" – the society – which in the boorish is "company" – of this male – which in the common is "boy"; which together is, abandon the society of this male, or, clown, thou perishest; or, to thy better understanding, diest; or, to wit, I kill thee, make thee away, translate thy life into death, thy liberty into bondage. I will kill thee a hundred and fifty ways! Therefore tremble and depart!!!

WILLIAM. God rest you merry, sir!

[MUSIC 14 – WILL U BE MY GROOM]

(**WILLIAM** *runs off.*)

(**TOUCHSTONE** *turns to* **ANDY.**)

ANDY. Touchstone!

TOUCHSTONE.
FROM THE MOMENT I SAW YOU, I KNEW.

ANDY.
YOU KNEW?

TOUCHSTONE.
ALL IT TOOK WAS JUST ONE SECOND TO KNOW
I WANNA MARRY YOU.
YOU'RE THE MOST PURE AND PERFECT ANDY
HEAVEN COULD BRING.

ANDY. Touchstone!

TOUCHSTONE.
I WOULD ONLY CHANGE A COUPLE THINGS.

(**ANDY** *gives an offended grunt.*)

NO OTHER MAN IS WORTHY
OF YOUR GORGEOUS FEATURES.

ANDY.

MY FEATURES?

TOUCHSTONE.

YOU DESERVE A DEVOTED ROMANCE
BABY, GIVE ME ONE MORE CHANCE

(**TOUCHSTONE** *gets down on one knee.*)

WILL YOU BE MY GROOM?
I'LL LOVE YOU RIGHT AND TRUE.
PLEASE MAKE ME THE HAPPIEST MAN AND SAY, "I DO!"
WILL YOU BE MY GROOM?
I'LL KEEP YOU SAFE FROM GLOOM.

TOUCHSTONE & ANDY.

WE'LL BE HAPPY EVER AFTER,
JUST JOY AND LAUGHTER.

ANDY.

WHEN WE RUN OFF IN THE SUNSET
AS THE PERFECT PAIR,

TOUCHSTONE.

THE PERFECT PAIR.

ANDY.

I'LL HOLD YOU IN MY ARMS
SO YOU KNOW I'LL BE THERE.

TOUCHSTONE & ANDY.

UNTIL THEY BURY ME IN MY TOMB,

TOUCHSTONE.

WILL YOU BE MY GROOM?

ANDY.

YES I WILL! YES I WILL! YES I WILL!

TOUCHSTONE.

WILL YOU BE MY GROOM?

ANDY.

YES I WILL! YES I WILL! YES I WILL!

TOUCHSTONE.

WILL YOU BE MY GROOM?

ANDY.

OH, YOU KNOW YEAH

I'M GONNA BE YOUR GROOM, TOUCHSTONE.

TOUCHSTONE.

ANDY, BE MY GROOM

TOUCHSTONE & ANDY.

DA DA DA DA DA DA DA OH

TOUCHSTONE.

WILL YOU BE MY GROOM?

ANDY.

GROOM?

TOUCHSTONE.

GROOM?

ANDY.

GROOM!

(**TOUCHSTONE** *and* **ANDY** *kiss and run off.*)

End of Scene

Scene Eighteen
In Arden, the Night Before the Wedding

(Enter **OLIVER** *and* **ORLANDO**, *with his arm in a sling.)*

ORLANDO. Is't possible that on so little acquaintance you should like her? That, but seeing, you should love her? And loving, woo? And wooing, she should grant?

OLIVER. Neither call the giddiness of it in question, but say with me "I love Aliena"; say with her that she loves me. It shall be to your good, for my father's house and all that was old Sir Rowland's will I estate upon you, and here live and die a shepherd.

(Enter **ROSALIND** *and* **CELIA**.*)*

ORLANDO. Let your wedding be tomorrow. Thither will I invite the Duke and all's contented followers. Go you and prepare Aliena, for, look you, here comes my Rosalind.

ROSALIND. *(As Ganymede, to* **OLIVER**.*)* God save you, brother.

OLIVER. And you, fair sister.

ROSALIND. *(As Ganymede.)* Did your brother tell you how I counterfeited to swoon when he showed me your handkerchief?

ORLANDO. Ay, and greater wonders than that.

ROSALIND. *(As Ganymede.)* O, I know where you are. For your brother and my sister no sooner met but they looked, no sooner looked but they loved, no sooner loved but they sighed, no sooner sighed but they asked one another the reason, no sooner knew the reason but they sought the remedy.

ORLANDO. They shall be married tomorrow. But O, how bitter a thing it is to look into happiness through another man's eyes.

ROSALIND. *(As Ganymede.)* Why, then, tomorrow I cannot serve your turn for Rosalind?

[MUSIC 15 – FOR REAL]

ORLANDO.
I DON'T WANT TO LIVE IN MY IMAGINATION.
I CAN'T PRACTICE ANY LONGER FOR THIS PART.
I WON'T SPEND ANOTHER SECOND
ON THE PAINT BY NUMBER PATTERN OF HER HEART.
YOU'VE TAUGHT ME HOW TO SEE
UNDERNEATH MY FANTASY
BUT THERE'S NOTHING LEFT
FOR ME TO LEARN IN THEORY.

I CAN'T GO ON THINKING.
NOW I NEED TO FEEL!
I'M READY TO LOVE HER FOR REAL.
IF ONLY SHE'D BE HERE FOR REAL.

ROSALIND. *(As Ganymede.)* I will weary you then no longer with idle talking. I know into what straits of fortune Rosalind is driven, and it is not impossible for me to set her before your eyes tomorrow, human as she is.

ORLANDO. Speak'st thou in sober meanings?

ROSALIND. *(As Ganymede.)* By my life I do.

*(Enter **SILVIA** and **PHOEBE**.)*

PHOEBE. Youth, you have done me much ungentleness
To show the letter that I writ to you.

ROSALIND. *(As Ganymede.)* I care not if I have.
You are there followed by a faithful shepherd.

[MUSIC 16 – GETTING MARRIED TOMORROW]

Look upon her, love her; she worships you.

PHOEBE. *(To **SILVIA**.)* Good shepherd, tell this youth what 'tis to love!

SILVIA.
> LOVE IS TREADING WATER
> IN A WHIRLPOOL OF YOUR TEARS
> AND SO AM I FOR PHOEBE!

PHOEBE.
> AND I FOR GANYMEDE!

ORLANDO.
> AND I FOR ROSALIND!

ROSALIND.
> AND I FOR NO WOMAN!

SILVIA.
> LOVE IS LETTING CUPID STAB YOU
> DAILY WITH HIS SPEARS,
> AND SO AM I FOR PHOEBE!

PHOEBE.
> AND I FOR GANYMEDE!

ORLANDO.
> AND I FOR ROSALIND!

ROSALIND.
> AND I FOR NO WOMAN!

SILVIA.
> LOVE IS GRIPPING ON TO HOPE
> SHE'LL REALIZE YOU'RE ALIVE!

ORLANDO.
> AND KNOWING THAT WITHOUT HER,
> YOU MAY NOT SURVIVE.

SILVIA.
> AND SO AM I FOR PHOEBE!

PHOEBE.
> AND I FOR GANYMEDE!

ORLANDO.
AND I FOR ROSALIND!

ROSALIND.
AND I FOR NO FEMALE HUMAN!

PHOEBE, SILVIA & ORLANDO.
SINCE YOU KNOW IT'S TRUE,
HOW CAN YOU BLAME ME FOR LOVING YOU?

ROSALIND. *(To* **ORLANDO.***)*
WHO ARE YOU TALKING TO?

ORLANDO.
TO HER THAT ISN'T HERE AND DOESN'T HEAR ME!

PHOEBE, SILVIA & ORLANDO.
SINCE YOU KNOW IT'S TRUE,
HOW CAN YOU BLAME ME FOR LOVING YOU?
LIKE I DO!

PHOEBE.
I DO!

SILVIA.
I DO!

ORLANDO.
I DO!

PHOEBE, SILVIA & ORLANDO.
I DO! I DO! I –

ROSALIND.
STOP!
I WILL HELP YOU IF I CAN,
SO LISTEN UP, HERE'S THE PLAN:

(To **PHOEBE.***)*

IF I EVER HAVE A WIFE, SHE'LL BE YOU.
AND I'M GETTING MARRIED TOMORROW.

(To **SILVIA**.*)*

IF SHE'S YOUR WISH, I'LL GRANT THAT TOO.
AND YOU'RE GETTING MARRIED TOMORROW.

(To **ORLANDO**.*)*

IF I EVER SATISFY A MAN, I'LL MAKE YOU GET YOUR WAY.
SO MEET ME HERE IN THE MORNING
FOR YOUR WEDDING DAY.

ORLANDO.

I'M GETTING MARRIED TOMORROW?

SILVIA & PHOEBE.

I'M GETTING MARRIED TOMORROW?

PHOEBE.

BUT –

ROSALIND.

DON'T ASK QUESTIONS, GIRL – JUST TRUST!

SILVIA, PHOEBE, ROSALIND & ORLANDO.

I'M GETTING MARRIED TOMORROW!

(The other **LOVERS** *join in.)*

CELIA & OLIVER.

I'M GETTING MARRIED TOMORROW!

ANDY & TOUCHSTONE.

I'M GETTING MARRIED TOMORROW!

JAQUES. Spoiler alert! It's a happy ending.

ROSALIND, ORLANDO, SILVIA, PHOEBE, CELIA, OLIVER, ANDY & TOUCHSTONE.

WE'RE ALL GETTING MARRIED TOMORROW!

(Meanwhile, back at the court, we see **DUKE FREDERICK** *and his* **ROYAL MINIONS**.*)*

A ROYAL MINION. Your Dukeness, we've just received news from Arden!

A ROYAL MINION.

YOUR DAUGHTER'S GETTING MARRIED TOMORROW!

A ROYAL MINION.

YOUR NIECE IS GETTING MARRIED TOMORROW!

A ROYAL MINION.

TO THE SONS OF SIR ROWLAND DE BOYS!

ALL ROYAL MINIONS.

THEY'RE ALL GETTING MARRIED TOMORROW!

DUKE FREDERICK. I will address a mighty power, and on foot, will take my brother in Arden, and put him to the sword!!

ALL ROYAL MINIONS.

YES, YOUR DUKENESS!

DUKE FREDERICK.

NO ONE'S GETTING MARRIED TOMORROW!
NO ONE'S GETTING MARRIED TOMORROW!
MOUNT YOUR HORSES, MEN – LET'S GO!
'CAUSE NO ONE'S GETTING MARRIED TOMORROW!

ROSALIND. Alright, everyone, we've gotta plan a quadruple wedding in under two minutes. Let's move, people!

*(The **ARDENITES** enter, making frantic preparations for the weddings.)*

HIGHER VOICES.

I'M GETTING MARRIED TOMORROW!

LOWER VOICES.

I'M GETTING

HIGHER VOICES.

I'M GETTING

ALL.

MARRIED TOMORROW!

TOUCHSTONE.
GET ME TO THE CHURCH ON TIME!

ALL.
I'M GETTING MARRIED TOMORROW!

HIGHER VOICES.
I'M GETTING MARRIED TOMORROW!

LOWER VOICES.
I'M GETTING

HIGHER VOICES.
I'M GETTING

ALL.
MARRIED TOMORROW!

LOWER VOICES.
WHO'S GETTING MARRIED?

HIGHER VOICES.
I'M GETTING MARRIED!

ALL.
I'M GETTING MARRIED TOMORROW!

HIGHER VOICES.
I'M GETTING MARRIED TOMORROW!

LOWER VOICES.
I'M GETTING

HIGHER VOICES.
I'M GETTING

ALL.
MARRIED TOMORROW!

ROSALIND.
MEET ME HERE AT DAWN.
NOW GO ON, GET GONE!

ALL.
> I'M GETTING MARRIED,
> I'M GETTING MARRIED,
> I'M GETTING MARRIED TOMORROW!
>
> *(Everyone skips happily off as they sing the last lines, leaving* **ROSALIND** *alone.)*

[MUSIC 17 – ROSALIND, BE MERRY (REPRISE)]

ROSALIND.
> IF HE'S READY TO LOVE YOU FOR REAL,
> WHY DO YOU FEEL THIS PAUSE?
> COME ON, ROZ...
>
> ROSALIND, BE MERRY.
> ROSALIND, BE SURE.
> YOU'RE ABOUT TO MARRY THE ONE PERSON YOU ADORE.
>
> ROSALIND, YOU'RE NERVOUS.
> ROSALIND, WHAT FOR?
> THERE'S NO REASON LEFT TO BE PERFORMING ANYMORE.
>
> SO WHY ARE YOU STILL UNDERNEATH THE COSTUME?
> UNDERNEATH THE COSTUME?
>
> GANYMEDE IS BRAZEN.
> HE IS IN CONTROL.
> GANYMEDE IS CANDID,
> BUT HE'S JUST ANOTHER ROLE.
>
> EASY TO BE CLEVER,
> HARDER TO BE TRUE.
> WILL YOUR LOVE SURVIVE IF YOU ARE NOBODY BUT YOU?
>
> *(She calls out to the forest.)*
>
> HEY, ARDEN,
> IF YOU HAVE A SERMON IN YOUR STONES.

THEN ARDEN, SPEAK THE LANGUAGE
OF MY HEART AND BONES.
OH ARDEN, HELP ME SEE THE LIGHT IN EV'RYTHING!
WHAT WAS IT I HEARD THEM SINGING?

ARDENITES. *(In the distance.)*
TOGETHER WE'LL HEAL OUR WOUND.
TOGETHER WE'LL HEAL OUR WOUND.

ROSALIND.
OUR WOUND,
OUR WOUND.

End of Scene

Scene Nineteen
The Weddings

*(**JAQUES** enters.)*

JAQUES. Hey, just a heads-up, the weddings are starting in like thirty seconds.

ROSALIND. We're getting married tomorrow.

JAQUES. Yeah well, you've been out here monologuing all night.

*(**ROSALIND** runs off in a hurry.)*

*(**TOUCHSTONE & ANDY, CELIA & OLIVER, SILVIA & PHOEBE, DUKE SENIOR, ORLANDO** and all the **ARDENITES** enter dressed up for the weddings.)*

TOUCHSTONE. Salutation and greeting to you all!

SILVIA. Today is the joyful day!

CELIA. *(To **OLIVER**.)* Today will we be married!

ANDY. I do desire it with all my heart!

DUKE SENIOR. Dost thou believe, Orlando, that the boy
Can do all this that he hath promised?

ORLANDO. I sometimes do believe and sometimes do not,
As those that fear they hope, and know they fear.

DUKE SENIOR. I do remember in that shepherd boy
Some lively touches of my daughter's favor.

ORLANDO. My lord, the first time that I ever saw him
Methought he was a brother to your daughter.
But, my good lord, this boy is forest-born!

[MUSIC 18 – FOR REAL (REPRISE)]

(**ROSALIND** *enters for the first time truly as herself.*)

ROSALIND.

ORLANDO, THERE'S SOMETHING YOU SHOULD KNOW:

ORLANDO. Ganymede?

ROSALIND.

ROSALIND.

ORLANDO.

ROSALIND?

ROSALIND.

I'M YOUR LOVER.

ORLANDO.

HE...

ROSALIND.

THE WHOLE TIME, IT'S BEEN ME.

ORLANDO.

YOU...?

TOUCHSTONE. I mean, did you seriously not realize it was her // all along?

ANDY. // Hush!

ORLANDO.

NO, I DIDN'T KNOW.
IT DOESN'T MATTER, THOUGH.
I CAN'T IMAGINE ANY LOVER
BUT YOU.

ROSALIND.

ME TOO.

ORLANDO. If there be truth in sight, you are my Rosalind.

ROSALIND. I'll have no husband if you be not he, Orlando.

ORLANDO.
I KNOW IT'S GOING TO TAKE WORK,
BUT I'M STILL PREPARED TO TRY.
AND I KNOW YOU'VE GOT YOUR SCARS,
WELL, SO DO I.

ROSALIND.
SO DO I.

ROSALIND & ORLANDO.
MAYBE TOGETHER, WE CAN GROW AND HEAL?
'CAUSE I'M READY TO LOVE YOU FOR REAL.
I'LL LOVE YOU FROM NOW ON FOR REAL.

> **(ROSALIND** *and* **ORLANDO** *kiss. Everyone cheers!)*

DUKE SENIOR. Rosalind! If there be truth in sight, you are my daughter!

ROSALIND. *(To* **DUKE SENIOR.***)* I'll have no father, if you be not he.

DUKE SENIOR. *(To* **CELIA.***)* O dear Celia, welcome thou art to me!

OLIVER. Celia?

CELIA. I shall explain later.

> **(PHOEBE** *steps forward, gesturing toward* **ROSALIND.***)*

[MUSIC 18A – YOU PHOEBE ME (REPRISE)]

PHOEBE.
SHE PHOEBE'D ME.
SHE PHOEBE'D ME.
SHE PHOEBE'D ME,
JUST LIKE I PHOEBE'D YOU.
I SHOULD BE THANKING GOD
FOR SENDING ONE SO TRUE,

'CAUSE NOBODY WILL EVER LOVE ME LIKE YOU DO.
YOU WANT ME.

SILVIA.
I WANT YOU.

PHOEBE.
YOU CHOOSE ME.

SILVIA.
I CHOOSE YOU.

PHOEBE.
AND I KNOW YOU WON'T REFUSE ME,
SO I'LL SILVIA YOU.

SILVIA.
YOU'LL SILVIA ME?

PHOEBE.
I'LL SILVIA YOU.

SILVIA.
OH SWEET PHOEBE!

(**SILVIA** *and* **PHOEBE** *kiss.*)

DUKE SENIOR. If any person present sees reason these couples should be not wed, speak now or forever hold your –

(*In storms* **DUKE FREDERICK,** *his* **ROYAL MINIONS,** *and* **BRONCO,** *swords raised. Everyone is scared silent at their presence.*)

[MUSIC 18B – ALL HAIL 4]

ROYAL MINIONS.
AH AH AH
ALL HAIL DUKE FRED'RICK!
AH AH AH
ALL HAIL DUKE FRED'RICK!

DUKE FREDERICK. Brother!

DUKE SENIOR. Brother?

[MUSIC 19 – UNDER THE GREENWOOD TREE (REPRISE)]

(**CELIA** *steps forward and* **DUKE FREDERICK** *sees her in her wedding dress.*)

(*Despite himself, he softens, surprised.*)

CELIA. Father?

DUKE FREDERICK. Celia!

(*Underneath this song, the redemptive power of Arden opens* **DUKE FREDERICK***'s heart.*)

(*He embraces his daughter,* **CELIA**, *and his brother,* **DUKE SENIOR**.)

(*He takes the crown off his head and places it on* **DUKE SENIOR***'s head.*)

(*By the end of the song, all is restored.*)

ALL (EXCEPT DUKE FREDERICK).
UNDER THE GREENWOOD TREE,
COME AND LIVE WITH ME
IF YOU WANT TO BE FREE
UNDER THE GREENWOOD TREE,

UNDER THE GREENWOOD TREE,
YOU SHALL SEE NO ENEMY,
YOU SHALL SEE NO ENEMY,
YOU SHALL SEE NO ENEMY,
DO NOT FEAR.
ALL ARE WELCOME HERE.
DO NOT FEAR.
ALL ARE WELCOME HERE

UNDER THE GREENWOOD TREE,
FORGIVE AND YOU'LL BE FREE, MY FRIEND.

IT'S NOT TOO LATE TO LOVE AGAIN.
IT'S NOT TOO LATE TO LOVE AGAIN.
IT'S NOT TOO LATE TO LOVE AGAIN.

DUKE SENIOR. Every of this happy number
That have endured shrewd days and nights with us
Shall share the good of our returned fortune.
Meantime, play, music!

[MUSIC 20 – STILL I WILL LOVE]

We'll so begin these rites,
As we do trust they'll end, in true delights.

(This song is the vows in the Ardenite community wedding ceremony, officiated by **DUKE SENIOR.***)*

ON THE HEAVIEST DAY,
ON THE BITTEREST NIGHT,

ALL.
STILL I WILL LOVE,
STILL I WILL LOVE.

DUKE SENIOR.
WHEN I'M TIRED AND HUNGRY,
AND WE'RE IN A FIGHT,

ALL.
STILL I WILL LOVE,
STILL I WILL LOVE.

DUKE SENIOR.
AS WE CHANGE AND WE GROW,
AS WE RIPEN AND ROT,

ALL.

    STILL I WILL LOVE,
STILL I WILL LOVE.

DUKE SENIOR.

    WHEN NOTHING TURNS OUT
QUITE THE WAY THAT WE THOUGHT,

ALL.

    STILL I WILL LOVE,
STILL I WILL LOVE
YOU.

DUKE SENIOR.

    WHEN I'M

ALL.

    SCARED TO LAY BARE
ALL THE PAIN IN MY CHEST,
STILL I WILL LOVE,
STILL I WILL LOVE.

DUKE SENIOR.

    AT OUR

ALL.

    BRAVEST AND WEAKEST,
OUR WORST AND OUR BEST,
STILL I WILL LOVE,
STILL I WILL LOVE.

DUKE SENIOR.

    WHEN WE

ALL.

    LOSE ALL OUR HAIR
AND OUR TEETH AND OUR MINDS,
STILL I WILL LOVE,
STILL I WILL LOVE.

DUKE SENIOR.

WHEN THE

ALL.

SCENERY FALLS
AND I MESS UP MY LINES,
STILL I WILL LOVE,
STILL I WILL LOVE.

DUKE SENIOR & 4 COUPLES.

I MAKE A PROMISE.

EVERYONE ELSE.

I MAKE A PROMISE

DUKE SENIOR & 4 COUPLES.

I MAKE A VOW

EVERYONE ELSE.

I MAKE A VOW

ALL.

TO MYSELF, TO YOU, TO EV'RYONE
RIGHT NOW.
WHEN THE WORLD TRIES TO TEAR US
APART AT THE SEAMS,
WHEN LIFE MAKES IT HARD
TO KEEP CHASING OUR DREAMS,
WHEN WE'RE MESSY AND WEEPY AND FEEBLE AND OLD,
WHEN WE DON'T HAVE A CLUE
WHAT THE FUTURE WILL HOLD...

DUKE SENIOR & EVERYONE ELSE.

STILL I WILL LOVE,

4 COUPLES.

STILL I WILL LOVE,

DUKE SENIOR & EVERYONE ELSE.

STILL I WILL LOVE.

4 COUPLES.
STILL I WILL LOVE.

DUKE SENIOR & EVERYONE ELSE.
STILL I WILL LOVE,

4 COUPLES.
STILL I WILL LOVE,

DUKE SENIOR & EVERYONE ELSE.
STILL I WILL LOVE.

DUKE SENIOR.   **4 COUPLES.**
OH,   STILL I WILL LOVE.

DUKE SENIOR & EVERYONE ELSE.
STILL I WILL LOVE,

ALL.
STILL I WILL LOVE
YOU.

(All couples embrace – they are now pronounced married!)

(The ceremony is over and now the reception begins!)

(Everyone joins in a raucous wedding dance!)

STILL I WILL LOVE, STILL I WILL LOVE.
STILL I WILL LOVE, LOVE!
STILL I WILL LOVE, STILL I WILL LOVE.
STILL I WILL LOVE, LOVE!
STILL I WILL LOVE, STILL I WILL LOVE.
STILL I WILL LOVE, LOVE!
STILL I WILL LOVE, STILL I WILL LOVE.
STILL I WILL LOVE, LOVE!

STILL I WILL LOVE!
STILL I WILL LOVE!
STILL I WILL LOVE!
STILL I WILL LOVE!
STILL I WILL LOVE!
STILL I WILL LOVE!
STILL I WILL LOVE!
STILL I WILL LOVE!

End of Scene

Scene Twenty
Epilogue

(Everyone jubilantly leaves the forest, heading home to the court to rebuild together.)

*(****ROSALIND**** and ****ORLANDO**** remain behind, still dancing in each other's arms.)*

[MUSIC 21 – EPILOGUE: ALL THE WORLD'S A STAGE]

DUKE SENIOR. Come, Jaques, come!

JAQUES. So to your pleasures. I am for other than dancing measures.

DUKE SENIOR. Jaques!

JAQUES. There is still much matter to be heard and learned out here.

DUKE SENIOR. Proceed, proceed.

*(****DUKE SENIOR**** exits.)*

JAQUES.

ALL THE WORLD'S A STAGE
ALL THE WORLD'S A STAGE

*(We see newlywed ****ROSALIND**** and ****ORLANDO**** grow older.)*

*(They're replaced by ****GRANDMA ROSALIND**** and ****GRANDPA ORLANDO****, older versions of themselves.)*

THEN WE GET OLDER
OUR MAKE-UP FADES AWAY.
OUR VOICES BECOME TIRED
AFTER ALL THE LINES WE DID OUR BEST TO SAY.

THEN OUR FINALE
STRUGGLING TO MAKE SENSE OF ALL WE'VE KNOWN.
WE LOOK AROUND THE THEATER
AND REALIZE WE'VE NEVER BEEN ALONE.

> (**GRANDMA ROSALIND** *and* **GRANDPA ORLANDO** *fade away, leaving* **JAQUES** *alone.*)

ALL THE WORLD'S A STAGE,
WHEN THE CURTAIN FALLS AT LAST,
THIS SHOW MUST STILL GO ON.
WE LEAVE A GHOSTLIGHT FOR THE ONES
WHO'LL START AGAIN WHEN WE ARE GONE.
WE LEAVE BEHIND THE SCENES AND STEPS
WE'VE LEARNED ALONG THE WAY
AND HOPE THEY LIVE TO SEE
A BETTER VERSION OF THE PLAY.

> (**JAQUES** *is replaced by a young girl,* **LITTLE JAQUES**, *who takes her pen and paper.*)

LITTLE JAQUES.
ALL THE WORLD'S A STAGE
AND EV'RYBODY'S IN THE SHOW.
NOBODY'S A PRO.
ALL THE WORLD'S A STAGE,
AND EV'RY DAY WE PLAY OUR PART,
ACTING OUT OUR HEART.
YEAR BY YEAR, WE GROW,
LEARNING AS WE GO,
TRYIN' TO TELL A STORY WE CAN FEEL.
HOW DO YOU MAKE THE MAGIC REAL?

JAQUES & LITTLE JAQUES.
LOVE MAKES MAGIC REAL.

The End

Scene Twenty-One
Bows

[MUSIC 22 – IN ARDEN (REPRISE)]

ALL.

IN ARDEN, OH IN ARDEN, OH IN ARDEN,
HOW SHALL WE LEARN TO BE?

LOWER VOICES.

HOW SHALL WE LEARN TO BE?

HIGHER VOICES.

IN ARDEN,

ALL.

OH IN ARDEN, OH IN ARDEN,
HOW SHALL WE LEARN TO BE?

IN ARDEN!

www.ingramcontent.com/pod-product-compliance
Lightning Source LLC
Chambersburg PA
CBHW070335120726
47909CB00008B/2696